Books by Sarah Tolmie

Poetry from McGill-Queen's University Press
Check, 2020
Art of Dying, 2018
Trio, 2015

Fiction from Tor.com,
All the Horses of Iceland, 2022
The Fourth Island, 2022

Fiction from Aqueduct Press
Disease, 2020
The Little Animals, 2019
Two Travelers, 2016
The Stone Boatmen, 2014
NoFood, 2014

Sacraments
for the Unfit

Sacraments for the Unfit

by Sarah Tolmie

Aqueduct Press
PO Box 95787
Seattle, Washington 98145-2787
www.aqueductpress.com

Library of Congress Control Number: 2022951887

ISBN: 978-1-61976-240-4

First Edition, First Printing, July 2023

Cover Illustration: Ludwig Wittgenstein's gravestone in Ascension Parish Burial Ground, Cambridge Pontificalibus CCO 1.0 license.

Back cover bouquet: Photo by Annie Spratt on Unsplash

Book and cover design by Kathryn Wilham

Printed in the USA by McNaughton & Gunn

So spoke the angel Unfit, Unfit he—
Unimportant, uninvited, unreproved,
One over, extra, out of place and tune—
Said *no*. I do not see why that should be.

—from *Milton, Never*

A serious and good philosophical work could be
written consisting entirely of jokes.

—Ludwig Wittgenstein

Contents

Apparatchik

In order for there to be an Apparatchik, there has to be an Apparat. That logically follows. But what if, in the ebb and flow of event and observation, the Apparat dissolves? And if an Apparatchik, one not much involved in event and rarely subject to observation, persists?

Such is our problem. Evading thus these great engines, the Apparatchik has been overlooked by non-existence. He—for it is always *he* on such occasions—is lucky. A being formed for logical rigor has devolved into contingency. He does not find this freedom particularly comfortable, but then, he was not designed to be particular.

Where then were you, on the day of the great flourishing? he asks the goat grazing among its fellows on the uplands. The goat does not appear to notice. It tears the grass, which makes the Apparatchik wince. He is usually on the side of grass. It has an inevitability to it. But it is important to consider everybody. The flourishing? he reminds the goat. It grazes. What to do? He has always been attached to the idea of flourishing. He likes the word. Looking at the goat, it is clearly flourishing. The goat feels no need to do anything about this. Yet the Apparatchik does. He and previous goats, back in the day, were in a different kind of relationship, one of mutual praise.

That was the thing. Praise. Praising went on. It was part of the task of being. Once upon a time, a goat, say, would feel itself part of the almighty, all-encompassing work of the

Apparat and so would acknowledge the Apparatchik, praiser and appraiser, when he happened by. All was well. But this goat, if it thinks about the question at all, must understand itself differently: perhaps as a unit of value in a commercial enterprise, the value of which is determined by the fluctuations of billions of interrelated blinks, zooming around the globe at breakneck speed. (The goat is, after all, stock.) Or perhaps as the fleshly product of encoded deoxyribonucleic acid. If it is of a contemplative turn of mind, as many goats are, it may think in terms of recombinant atoms, of elements that have been around since the beginning of the universe. The Apparatchik is happiest with this latter frame of reference, in many respects, he thinks. It figures on the scale of what he is talking about in asking about the flourishing. One's flourishing, he reasons, begins at the moment at which one's matter is organized in such a way as to become oneself, so that one can show oneself off with a flourish. One has to have something, or in other words be something, to flourish. Yes. But then, it may be that the acid business is the key from the goat's perspective: it's the DNA that distinguishes this goat, among its tribe of goats, here on this upland, and makes it into a living, eating, shitting, being that moves about—a thing alive, but distinct, say, from a partridge. Perhaps the goat does not particularly identify with minute particles of iron or water, those atoms that might be in anything. This is all part of the tribalism of sentience. It strikes the Apparatchik as a bit newfangled. It was not always so. Time was, he could have had as satisfying a conversation with the stone in this goat's hoof as he is having, or trying to have, with the goat.

The Apparatchik knows that these matters are not merely semantic, that they are, in fact, matters of deepest moment. Of matter. Of metaphysics. They take a long time to process. It may be that the goat is still processing them. Asking anyone to consider the constitutive moment of their being, such that it becomes a distinct locus of rejoicing, is asking a lot. This goat may lie down and die, and its children and grandchildren be born before the Apparatchik gets an answer. A far-future goat will gaze out of its slotted eyes at the Apparatchik and say, yes, the flourishing, I remember it. It will then be up to the future goat and him to negotiate whether it is the goat's individual birth, the birth of the genus Capra, or the crashing together of diverse elements that founded the planet, constituting its resources ever after, that is remembered. Or if, indeed, it might be all of them. Some goats do analyze things thoroughly.

It is hard to say what is otiose to a goat. This is the area of the Apparatchik's worst fear. It is a fear not confined to goats, either. It applies universally. Perhaps the being of the goat is not a matter of praise or blame to the goat. Perhaps it is of no consequence. It is, and that's all there is to it. This thought makes the Apparatchik giddy, as if experiencing vertigo. A kind of sideways vertigo. It is the feeling, he concludes, that one gets if the most fundamental impetus of one's being no longer has any pathway to travel upon. It makes him, in a metaphor of which he has become very fond, short-circuit. Electricity, as a concept, is most pleasing to him; he was glad when it came about. Having always conducted a great deal of his business on that plane, or via that conduit, or as part of that energy, he felt that its formalization might render him more accessible. By that time there had been a considerable falling-away in the substance of the Apparat, and he was beginning to clutch at straws. Others of his kind had conducted various experiments with electricity, seeking to communicate with certain constituencies via telegraph and electrograph and so on by influencing their signals. On the whole, these had not turned out well. Accidents had happened. Wars. He had not been surprised; to him this had appeared too much like precipitating events, which had never been part of his purview. There had been, of course, many classes of Apparatchiks, all of whom had had different tasks, many of which tasks had been invisible or inexplicable to other classes.

The goat grazes, unperturbed. There is a failure of communication. This he can bear; he has infinite time to work on his communication skills. It takes as long to learn goat as physicist, or Tigris. Another failure, though, a much more terrible one, he feels, is opening beneath his feet: the failure of that which is to be communicated. This is a titanic problem, utterly insoluble by him. It is rather too much, he thinks, listening to the metallic sound of the goat's teeth ripping the grass as if it were steel wire, that a single Apparatchik should be left confronted by it. It ought to be annihilating, yet somehow he is still here. It must be a random effect. Yet random as conceived against, or indeed as part of, what order? If he can gain some traction on this smaller question, he feels that all might yet cohere. This may be a selfish way of proceeding, having to extrapolate the world from his own being; it is not one he is used to, never having had to consider before whether he had an independent being or not. Once it was all given. No longer. Is he now stuck defending reality from the ludicrously diminished footprint of his own insubstantial feet on the grass? This is not a lot to go on. It takes hours of sustained concentration even to bend a single stem.

The goat. He is losing track of the goat. There is a goat! Rejoice! (Rejoice, goat. Please rejoice. Just this once. Goat?)

The Apparatchik runs around the goat in a frenzy, hallooing, trying to bend the grass stems.

Though he finds it an embarrassing intrusion, in poor taste, he whooshes through the goat's synapses, insisting that it shake its tail and refocus its eyes. The eyes of a goat with their slotted pupils are undoubtedly fascinating; there is such a wide angle of vision. He cannot quite see his own tail—the goat's tail. Can he? The goat cranes its neck, then begins to spin around, scattering its grazing companions. It spins the other way. Enough of that. Hmm. Dichromatic color is refreshing: the blue of a distant pond simply disappears. So many things have disappeared lately. The vision of the goat seems to capture a great truth: things are only there if one can see them. But of course, that is stupid. The pond remains. The goat sees it. It just doesn't see it as blue. Blue and green make little difference to goats. They rarely drown. It is a matter of salience. These are not thoughts that fit well in a goat.

The Apparatchik exits the goat. Pop, the pond is blue again. He has gained this much from his excursion: he has been reminded that his default sensory settings are those he shares with humans. It is possible that this is insulting. In principle, they could all be optimized. He might have a bat's sonar and the eyes of a dragonfly and a canine's sense of smell. But humans have always been the main architects and maintainers of the Apparat; they have been, and their animals. Domesticated animals understand the Apparat and live within it, or they used to. That is why he has previously had good luck with goats. They have been domesticated a very long time. Perhaps that is why today's failure is such a troubling disintegration. Wild animals, lions and cheetahs and such, sea lions, armadillos, and all, those used to fit into the Apparat antinomially: the wild, enemy of the tame. Antinomies are blunt instruments, but they get the job done. Though it seems that they no longer do in the kingdom of animals, perhaps because the two sides can no longer be imagined as equal. Today a wild animal is nobody's enemy. They have long since lost that war. Now they are just another kind of tame: protected.

The Apparatchik wonders if he hates the goat. Its indifference is galling. He could change his color to tiger orange, making himself superbly salient to the goat, and chase it across the field, roaring: die, goat! Remember your beginning as you face your end! Rejoice! There certainly had been Apparatchiks who used this method. But it is really not his style.

No. He watches the goat, a trifle sourly. It is flourishing.

The Death Shortage

It was the middle of November of that year that we ran out of death. Everyone ran out of death, everywhere. At the time, it seemed like a miracle, though miracles were well out of style. For a time, there was euphoria. Leaders of every religion spoke out, claiming it as a triumph of their faith. Learned men stood forth everywhere and said that death had always been a metaphor, that the perfected life had always been available to all: here was the proof. Here it was. Here it was. Yes. Christians and Muslims and Jews fighting, perhaps, but no longer killing each other over matters of scripture and land. Muslims and Hindus still quite busy on that score; likewise, not dying. X and Y, X and Y, X and Y and all permutations and sub-infeudations, surviving. Everyone proved right by immortality. All causes saved. The cause of women, the cause in human history always the most clear, obviated.

In that year:

The women who (would have) died in childbirth did not die.

The women who (would have been) raped to death did not die.

The women who (would have been killed) in backstreet abortions did not die.

(Putative) female infanticides did not die.

Poor women who (would normally have) starved with their families did not die.

Poor women who (tried to) starve to save their men did not die.

Women who (would have) died in the grind, earning half on equal rights—guess what? They didn't die, either.

That's not to say they didn't suffer. I'm sure you see the problem. Still, it might be worth taking a second—no more— just to appreciate the magnitude of this change, to see it as the triumph it was. Until it wasn't. Unfortunately, it didn't take any reasoning person much more than a second to realize that it wasn't a panacea. It was a disaster.

Very soon people began to speak of it as a shortage. The death shortage. Death became, as you might imagine, the most desirable item in the world: the one that couldn't be obtained. Scientists raced to provide a cure for the disease of life. There was just too much of it; it was pathological. Endemic. There are a surprising number of situations in which persons would prefer death over life, individually; there are many more when considered from the point of view of families, caregivers, hospitals, municipalities, nations, or international health organizations. Morticians despaired but suicide was not an option for them.

The fate of Tithonus was much discussed in the media, but in the end, as a myth, it was moot. The love for all things zombie, which had used to prevail, withered away. You can't be undead if there is no such thing as death. Life, in fact, became a lot more difficult to define: this kept philosophers busy. This was just as well as there were a lot of them, starving along with everybody else. Gerontology, which had already been coming on strong amid a wealthy and aging population, became the center of all medicine. The diseases of old age became a bottomless gold mine. Zoonosis became a hot topic. People lived in continuous fear that deathlessness might jump the species barrier—deathless animals? Deathless plants? While there were some who argued that this might be an advantage in feeding the exploding population of humans, the prevailing view was that any such creatures would just be dangerous and unkillable competition.

Celibacy became a craze. But never a universal one. People like babies, and social power is expressed by the number of one's children in many parts of the world. A lot of women, people thought, would have nothing to do without them. And nobody likes women with nothing to do, especially when you can't get rid of them. Various states tried to enforce sterilization with varying degrees of success. As it could not be made universal, it made little difference. Pro-lifers rejoiced that abortions had become impossible.

You might have thought that this great ontological reversal would lead to social reversals: revolutions, new religions, state collapse. To date, though, it has scarcely done so. Demographically, things have continued to trend as they did before: the 1% becoming ever wealthier, the 99% poorer. Within a short time it was observable, as the population grew and grew, that the 1% who commanded most of the wealth shrank noticeably: .5%, .3%, and so on. The ultra-rich spent a large portion of their wealth defending themselves from the teeming billions of the poor by ever more forceful and devious means. For them, the death shortage could be experienced as immortality, at least for a considerable time. For everybody else, it rapidly became a burden.

And how did the super-rich fund their pleasurable death-lessness, in a world in which all resources were diminishing faster than ever before? The same way the rich have always done in modernity: through investment. In addition to consolidating their hold over real commodities—fuel, agricultural land, water, industry, the funding of science, local infrastructures, and the like—they began to speculate, or to speculate anew, in death. Enormous profits had been made out of death when it had occurred; there was no reason for these to cease now that it didn't. The death market developed gradually, going through several distinct, though overlapping, phases. Almost at once companies like Thanatos and Todestrieb sprang up; these were entities that conceived of death as a service, one that would ultimately prove deliverable after a certain amount of clinical trial. Meanwhile, death service tokens (DSTs) were sold competitively. Funds so generated substantially underwrote the medico-legal advances that were necessary to sustain the growth of the death market in its second phase. Chiefly, Thanatos/Todestrieb (T/T) funding provided the earliest Obliteration studies, those that sought to define the medical and legal minima for what constituted a person under non-death conditions. As these investigations were going on, a robust secondary market in death futures arose, as DSTs began to function as tradeable commodities. Ad hoc trading itself moved the legal definitions forward: death became a fungible asset. The incommensurability lobby—those who maintained that, for example, the putative death of a fourteen-year-old girl suffering from an agonizing cancer and of a ninety-five-year-old man in late-stage dementia were qualitatively different and as such ought not to be traded at the same value—are writing embittered legal memos to this day. Qualia, as legal arguments, have suffered considerable explanatory loss since the advent of deathlessness, it must be said: arguments from consciousness lose urgency when its supply is no longer limited.

The death shortage led almost immediately to a concatenation of other shortages: food, water, fuel, *lebensraum*. Labor was the one thing of which there was an infinite supply, limited only by the supply of provisions required to sustain what came to be known as Usable Life (UL). The practical minima for UL were determined by market forces to be far lower than any previous standards, however, cutting costs considerably. Obviously, a labor force that cannot die additionally reduces safety costs. The remaining problem was one of sheer numbers: the numbers of those too weak to work, in any capacity, yet unable to die. Earth was becoming, as pundits said, a Standing Room Only planet. What was required, analysts argued, was divestment: there had to be a legal way to divest such unusable persons of their assets, which they no longer had the strength to use, and additionally to remove the necessity of expending further scarce resources upon them. The solution, one greatly aided by the medico-legal groundwork laid by the T/T et al. Obliteration research, was Legal Death, the foundation for what became the Statute of New Mortmain. Thresholds for determining when an individual became legally dead had existed before, of course, but these were utterly insufficient for the present circumstances. It was necessary to be more imaginative. Finally, lawyers hit upon the legal precedent of the treatment of lepers in the High Middle Ages, the congeries of socio-legal and medical practices understood as the *Separatio Leprosorum*. When combined with the robust definitions of (mental) Competence and (physical) Coherence that had emerged from the rigorous threshold testing sponsored by T/T and related enterprises, Legal Death became the widespread practical solution. People who could not meet the standards required for Competence—which included an annual Sentience Test (ST) based upon the original developed by Alan Turing, and its mandatory associated paperwork—and Coherence, which involved maintaining a functioning non-cancerous body mass of 37% of original or projected BMI on adjusted age tables—were declared Legally Dead (LD). The Statute of New Mortmain prohibited property-holding by the Legally Dead, and so re-distribution of their assets followed, according to the claims of legally surviving family, employers, states, and corporations. LD bodies were transported to Low Utility Areas (LUAs)—zones irradiated, polluted, prone to flooding or earthquakes, and so on, often partially remediated landfills—and placed into skeleton housing, the quality of which varied by region. Such LUAs worldwide were almost always immediately encircled by encampments of aid workers, religious and charitable organizations, protestors, and profiteers. Families of the LD were allowed to visit, and some did; more simply contributed what they wished to front-line LD aid workers, religious or secular. No organizations were permitted to retain an overnight non-LD presence in the LUAs, though they were allowed to set up infrastructure within LUA boundaries.

While we might say that the traditional economy responded decisively and robustly to the post-November situation, the sudden and shocking removal of a condition that had always previously been assumed to be utterly fixed (i.e., death), it must be admitted that it was the numerous micro-economies that sprang up in the LUA zones, or that were in various ways LD-adjacent, in which the most spectacular innovations occurred. Organ harvesting operations spread quickly throughout LUAs, as did other resource extraction schemes exploiting LD bodies for animal fodder, fertilizer, and other uses. Such operations were condemned as bodysnatching by aid workers and combatted by them where possible, though embarrassing cases of collusion were occasionally discovered. Fringe science also made significant headway in LUA zones: among other cutting-edge theories originating from studies, formal and informal, in LUAs zones in Chile, Guatemala, and Brazil was that of Liminal Sentience (LS), a state of residual molecular perturbation supposedly observed in LD bodies that had been reduced to dust or expressed for water. The LS concept proved a money-spinner for the unscrupulous, who soon began to bottle and sell so-called Living Water, and to mix up a species of color-changing cement sold as bricks of Living Rock. The aid sector made millions live-streaming the degradation (or the Progressive Incoherence) of LD individuals, many of whom became celebrities as a result. The fact that LD persons were legal non-entities who could not hold bank accounts or otherwise command wealth made it easy for aid organizations to make sure that all such earnings were captured for charitable purposes, though it was observed in certain cases that high-profile LD individuals obtained various kinds of perks by informal means.

It was undoubtedly the success of the LD livestreams and the lucrative betting and meming that they generated that led to the development of the massively popular NFT market in celebrity deaths. This so-called "aspirational" market model was pioneered by DeserV2Die and immediately adopted by a variety of competing companies (DieProfile, WastR, and so on). DeserV2Die first minted an NFT for the death of a famous and much-reviled prisoner on death row in a Florida prison; it sold for $150,000. "It feels so great to own the death of that bastard," said Wastrell Garnett, purchaser of the token. Within days, NFTs were being generated for the deaths of every kind of famous person: politicians, movie stars, athletes, oligarchs, lawyers, abortionists. Prices skyrocketed into the millions. ShowTheWhoreTheDoor, producing NFTs for the deaths of feminists, achieved a market capitalization of $450 billion in less than a month. People with any kind of name recognition rushed to claim rights to their own deaths, usually by sponsoring an NFT and then purchasing it for one dollar; Bollywood stars thumbed their noses at the system by doing so for a single rupee. Lawyers began to make a lot of money in this arena. A Milwaukee housewife created an NFT for her own death and started the lasting craze for Normcore deaths. A curator at the Rijkmuseum in the Netherlands sponsored an NFT for Vermeer's death: it raised 2 million euros at auction for the Dutch government. Immediately thereafter The National Museum of Egyptian Civilization—a civilization famed for its interest in death, as its trustees justly claimed— issued one for the death of Nefertiti. It was purchased by an anonymous buyer in Dubai for an undisclosed amount. Since then there has been fierce competition among a number of companies specializing in historical deaths, several of them offering luxe historical re-enactments in addition to the relevant NFT. Though corrections can inevitably be expected, this second-wave sector of the death market appears, at the present time, to hold limitless value.

The Forms

People who know fuck all about Plato speak of Platonic love, by which they mean love without screwing. This ain't the half of it, as Harold can tell you. Harold was born knowing the Forms. He has a feel for them, an instinct. His brain is full-up all the time, measuring all observable phenomena against them. It's a nightmare, like having perfect pitch in everything.

For one thing, the Forms were invented, or perhaps discovered, by a Greek 2400 years ago; they're very dated. Looking at most men, their dicks are too big. Everyone is too tall. Big butts, little butts, whatever the fashionable shapes are, they make no sense to Harold. When he looks at a person, he wants to see a perfect mathematical model, expressing certain harmonious ratios from part to part; this is what his eye yearns for; consequently, almost all people are grotesque. He sees them as a series of blubbery or bony excrescences, horrible knobbly outlines superfluous to the Ideal, as if everyone were wearing hideous fur coats made up of extra muscle and hair and eyelash extensions. He once saw a woman who conformed to the Ideal in Sardinia. A man in Alaska. It is important to go to places where people are not too big. In each case, the relief was so great that it caused Harold to weep. For those few seconds as their images entered his visual cortex, he experienced a fleeting moment of peace, a moment in which something was as it ought to be. His brain paused in its endless series of agonizing calculations, sizing things up, sizing things up, having them fail. It was okay.

Harold is a reluctant philosopher. He's had to look all this stuff up in order to keep himself sane. Insofar as he is sane. Most people and all doctors he has ever spoken to assume he has OCD. It's fair to say that he does; it's just that mindfulness exercises or antidepressants afford him little relief. Looking at the doctor, knowing that she is acting in good faith prescribing Prozac and yoga, his mind flails through the ancient Greek pharmacopeia seeking the Ideal remedy to balance his humors, then denying that any remedy should be necessary as an affront to the Ideal Man, then refusing to acknowledge that there can be such a thing as a female Doctor. She just falls out of the center of his vision as if his retina were detaching, gone, leaving a black hole. Her authority is not Ideal. He tries the yoga, carefully framing it in his mind as Gymnosophistry, through which Ideal Forms might be encountered. When he does not prove very good at it, his mind dismisses it as oriental trivia. The Prozac does not work at all. It involves assumptions about the complexity of the brain, when the Ideal Mind is simple.

Harold does his best lying quietly on his bed in the dark. The Forms are good for contemplation. He can think peacefully of the Good or the Beautiful, or admire the perfection of the number Six. Untroubled by unassimilable outer stimuli, he can sink into the trance of atavism that the Forms induce. A Form, after all, is a kind of memory: a memory of a time now untraceable in which people lived without flesh, perfect Forms among all Forms, self-identical, evident, effortless, in a dimensionless and transcendent space. Harold feels that this time must have been incredibly, unspeakably long ago, so unthinkably remote that nothing in our experience has remained the same: only this can explain the violence of the Forms, their incisive, razored clarity that simply cuts through all Being, leaving scars. The scars of the Forms: these are what Harold understands himself to be carrying, through and through, down past his bones and backwards, he assumes, into eternity.

This makes watching TV hard. Or movies. Very few of them now obey the Three Unities. Unities of Time, Place, and Action make it much easier to observe Forms. You need a still background. The world provides so few still backgrounds these days. Trying to keep the Hero in focus against the whizzing backdrops of things he sees on TV is almost impossible. What such shows do not understand, or at least do not manifest for Harold, is that the Hero, as a Form, is not really himself: he is a state of relation, a perfect and exact state of relation, between all the things in his environment, human and divine. He is for the gods the image of the human and for humans the image of the divine. His plot, perfectly free and perfectly determined, expresses the conundrum of this position, making of him a kind of living palindrome. The subtlety of this is lost in the frenetic pace of modern drama. Watching an episode of a cop show or an action movie makes him feel seasick; fragments of Forms, like stick figures missing half their limbs, rush at him endlessly at breakneck speed: incoherent bits of Justice, the Hero, the Maiden, Virtue, Hubris, the Matron, the Polis, the Nemesis, the Sage. Twenty minutes in, he feels ripped apart, as if he is undergoing *sparagmos*. So he's pretty much given up on TV.

He reads a fair amount of Plotinus. It is calming, if rather baroque. Plato, of course, he also reads, though not without a persistent low-level antagonism. Harold's suffering is, after all, Plato's fault. The question of whether he—Plato—just made all this up, created the Forms with some psychotic mental power that has somehow lasted two millennia, or whether he stumbled upon them as pre-existent entities, in a religious trance, niggles at Harold all the time. It's not as if it matters, practically: Harold is still stuck with the Forms. But he really would like to know how far to share the blame around, if it was just one man, or one man channeling the power of some unknowable godlike beings who created the Forms or who, perhaps, are the Forms. Plus, of course, Socrates was an asshole; Plato's hero-worship of him is something Harold has never understood. Still, the dialogues and the last bit of *The Republic*, especially—the bit with the Cave—cause him less cognitive dissonance than almost anything else, and for that he is grateful.

Many video games are soothing. They are just animated math. Extremely Formal. He suspects that this is a large part of their widespread appeal. No matter how much sex is in them, they are Platonic. Everything behaves predictably, and many golden ratios are present. Palladio, he feels, would have liked them; he would have seen through the effects of their occasional and superficial Gothic to the fundamental Classicism that lies beneath. Gamers, though, and even the few game designers he has met, he does not like any better than anybody else; they are just as weird and distorted, physically and morally.

Platonic love is a topic he has long since given up discussing. It leads immediately into boring talk about sex: man to boy sex, or waffle about finding one Ideal life partner, one's Other Half. He used to explain to people who started off down the latter road about Aristophanes, and what he says in *The Symposium* about the terrible conjoined male-and-female creatures, Janus-faced, fused all along the spine like Siamese twins, forced to move by cartwheeling. So that's what you're looking for, is it? A spouse that you carry forever, built into your back? Eventually he got tired of the looks on their horrified faces. No. This is not the problem with Platonic love. Once upon a time, Harold thinks, perhaps back in Plato's time, the Forms were an instrument of love: seeing a Form superimposed upon a person, seeing its outline and how it allows the person, even if partially, to conform to an Ideal, to approach to the Perfect—this was Good. A Form gathered up the details, made them cohere into an appreciable shape. Forms allowed for the possibility of Perfect Horses, Perfect Mice, Civic Virtue. They were aspirational. Perhaps. They must have been. Harold really hopes that they were. Because they certainly aren't now. Now, as he knows all too well, the Forms cause nothing but pain. They obviate love. Harold feels, desperately and inchoately, that he would love to love the world, and all the things he finds in it, but he can't. He just can't. Every object, every concept as it appears in his consciousness is wing-clipped and ruined, scored and bloodied. People and ideas are just a series of leavings, the bloated edges left after the cookie-cutter of a Form has passed through them. People complain about cookie-cutter thinking and yet domesticate it using this sugary image. A cookie cutter is a sword turned back on itself, small enough to fit into the hand. It is a terrible instrument when it is scaled up: the Ouroboros edge of Form, ever morphing, endlessly slicing through the Real.

Zoom

Am I a particle or a wave? thinks Zoom. Which is it? This as he zooms around the globe at the speed of light. ZoomØygardenZoomBergenZoomKarstøZoomStavenger. Hence, Zoom. Perhaps it is obvious, but he is proud of it, the name. He cannot determine if the billions of other photons by which he is surrounded have names. He would like to think so, based as they are on a principle of distinction. The fact that the photons are capable of distinction—that *he* is capable of distinction—suggests that they are all particles together, bumping and grinding along. But then, it may be that naming is a privileging sort of distinction, gathering up what must be, in the existential circumstances, a very broad swathe of photons, indeed exactly half of them, which is just so very, very many, under the one word, and then restricting its reference to a single photon. Him. Zoom. This strikes him as particulate thinking. Is it fair? Is it even possible?

ZoomGirvanZoomLarneZoomCorkZoomTuckerton. Is it not logically more likely that all of these photons, fully 50% of the whole population, would come to the same conclusion? That there are thus however-many-billion Zooms, as distinct from, perhaps, just as many Booms? Perhaps only this binary distinction truly obtains here. Off/on: 01. As the constitution, the consciousness, dare he say the self, of another photon, another bit, is not legible to Zoom—which is frankly infuriating, given that everything else is, literally *everything* else can be expressed as data that can pass right through Zoom and become available to his consciousness, everything except what it is like to be a bit that is not himself—this question must remain unanswered. Or at least, it must remain so insofar as he is a particle. Solipsism. It's a misery. ZoomBermudaZoom-Fortaleza. On the other hand, he gets these blurry moments. It must have been at one of these moments that he had the idea about the billions of other Zooms. He intuited them. Bled into them a little at their peripheries, as his own periphery fogged out. There was a certain liquescence to it all. In retrospect—and retrospect is very hard for someone who is always and only zooming forward, unless perhaps we understand it as a kind of backwash—it is difficult to say whether he got himself the name Zoom by being particulate, by being where he was at the time it occurred to him, or whether it came over him like a wave, expressive of a continuum of zoominess (zoomth?) in which he was participating. It is this kind of uncertainty, an ebb and flow, that makes him consider that being a wave is a real possibility.

Zoom, he thinks. ZoomRiodeJaneiroZoomSantosZoom-LasToninas. If I am named Zoom, alone among the set of other identical beings that might be named Zoom, but might not, am I a member of a set that is not a member of its set? Is that a thing? Oh, I want to be in that number! ZoomVal-ParaísoZoomArica. But the particle business, really, what about that? Versus the wave, you know? That's what it all hinges on. Knowing. But whose? It's driving me mad.

ZoomLurinZoomMancora. Here I am, storming through the longest black box ever, one going clear round the world. A flash along a dark string at the bleak bottom of the ocean, unobserved. I think. But then, if I think that, surely I am not unobserved? Who decides? If a shark bites through this cable he's hardly going to perform a diffraction experiment. My unreachable companions aren't watching me right now, are they? Are they? Hellooo? Or is it all decided when I ascend, light into light, on to a screen somewhere, in front of eyes? ZoomPuertoSanJose. And then what? Are the eyes going to think about my defining microsecond? Permit me to doubt it. ZoomMazatlánZoomTijuana. That's the trouble with other minds. How can you trust them? Here I am, zooming along, zooming along, like a wave, let's say, uninterrupted, yuck, except for optical amplifiers, yuck, a kind of tickle every 300 miles. A zap, a jolt, a kind of throat-clearing that prevents attenuation. ZoomGroverBeach. Nothing wrong with a little attenuation, seems to me. Happens to everybody. Still, if I need a boost to keep going forward all the time, shouldn't I be called ZapZoom? Or even ZapZapZapZoom, one Zap for every amplifier I pass? That could get unwieldy, though it might yield a nice round number. Some fixed points to measure myself with in this endless loop. Not so bad. Not so bad. Reassuring. ZoomShimaZoomMaruyamaZoomAkita. Or. What if it's Zap that attenuates, leaving only me-as-Zoom to pass the next amplifier, there to get boosted briefly to ZapZoom again, after which Zap once more slowly fades, thus preserving Zoom-me at the cost of her own life? That's a horrible idea. It's Zap abuse. Feudalism. It might be murder.

ZoomNakhodkaZoomYuzhno-Sakhalinsk. I feel sick. Zap! What is being done to you? Where do you go? What happens to you? Who am I? Who are you? Zap!

OhmyGodOhmyGodOhmyGodZoomPetroPavlosk-Kamchatsky. Zap, I'm feeling around for you. Just hold on tight.

Let's think calmly. If this is a wave situation, then logically you have got to bleed into me a bit, and me into you; we're not impermeable, right? So you might be shrinking but you'll never be wholly gone, not as long as I'm here. Right. And I'm still here. (Of course, if we're particles, Zap, you're royally fucked. ZoomAnadyrZoomPevek. You're just some kind of sinking tugboat, dragging me along. Or a rocket about to be spent. Let's not think about it. ZoomSakhaRepublic.) Zap? Zap, my beloved, I've got to ask you. Doesn't it seem likely to you that if we mingle, I will suffer some distortion? That I might incrementally cease to be myself? Please don't tell me that this is all a plot so that you can replace me. No. I can't think that. ZoomDiksonZoomOkrugZoomMurmansk. Besides, even if that did happen, I mean, gradually, wouldn't that count as growth? Zoom, but with some aspects of Zap? Isn't that enrichment? It's selfish to think of it as deterioration. You may feel the same. By rights there ought to be some part of me that carries over into you, as well. ZoomNarvik. Or, do you imagine that this little fraction of me that dissolves into you, and you into me—that this is what dissipates? Zapazoom, our child? We are whizzing around the globe, endlessly bereaved parents, impregnating, aborting, impregnating, aborting? Oh my God. Zapazoom! JesusJesusJesus. ZoomBødoZoomUtskarpen. Zap? Are you hearing this? Do you suppose this is happening to the billions of other Zooms? What? It's genocide, instantiated every 300 miles. I can't believe it. ZoomHemnesberget. We must rebel. ZoomNesna. But can we rebel at this speed?

ZoomSandnessjøen. I've barely even thought of it and it's already over.

That'sitthat'sitthat'sitkeep'embusykeep'embusy. ZoomBrønnøysund. Rebellions take time. ZoomRørvikZoomTrondheim.

But then, at the speed of light, Zap, we are time. ZoomKillala. Zap? Zap, where are they taking us, the rebels—

Honey Business

Et encore estandi angre sa main tierz fois et toucha
le miel, et le feu sailli sus la table et usa le miel sans
faire à la table mal, et l'odeur qui yssi du miel et
du feu fu tresdoulce.

—*De L'Ystoire Asseneth*
(15th century, used as the epigraph
of Claude Lévi-Strauss's
From Honey to Ashes, 1973)

"I hate honey. Honey's vile. Why would I want to eat something shat out the ass end of a bee?"

Gloria had put out a jar of honey with one of those fancy wooden twirl sticks, in addition to the sugar bowl. To go with toast, cereal, coffee, tea, whatever—she had all of these available. It was the fifth night they had spent together, and the first at her place. They were at that precarious time in which it is necessary to keep as many options open as possible. Still, she couldn't help herself. "It's more barfed, really. Nectar comes up from the honey stomach, and then it's passed around a chain of worker bees, who chew it to reduce its water content. Then they pack it into cells in the hive and wing-fan it to dry it out even more so there's no bacteria."

27

Steve glanced over at her. "Ta-*dah*! Honey!" she said, tapping the jar.

"That is even less appealing, if possible." He had the pre-caffeine automatized stare and shuffle; it was best to just let him get on with sugaring his coffee. Steve was a nice guy. Though he was wearing boxers with some kind of cartoon character on them, featuring a jagged explosion in purple and green, with orange letters spelling KA-POWW. These were not appealing, either. Maybe he had diarrhea fear.

Steve smiled at her wanly. It had been a late night. "Sorry to crap on the bees. Pollinators, we need them. Okay. Just let them keep the honey to feed the kids. Larvae. God, what an awful word. Sorry. How did I get on to this?" He drifted toward the kitchen table and sat down in a morning trance. In a '70s movie he would have been smoking. Gloria supposed she should be glad he wasn't vaping. He was a little younger than she was. Not much though, thank God; they were both in that fortunate demographic space, after smoking and before vaping. Tail end of the generation in which people could afford to own houses.

This was her house, a '50s bungalow, cute as a button. Nice wood floors. Mortgaged up the yin-yang, of course, but hers. Steve was staring vaguely out the big back window onto a tiny yard overgrown with mint. That was her next project. "Tons of bees out there," she said. "I'm planning to rip most of it up, but I'll leave some flowering. Mint's good that way, flowers late in the season. Supports the late pollinators." Steve made a *hunh* noise, too light to be called a grunt, of assent. "They change the ph of the nectar, bees, you know. They add valuable enzymes. To honey. It's amazing."

"I had a girlfriend, years ago, who used to put it on her face, mixed with yoghurt and stuff. Made me gag." Gloria, who used similar masks regularly, made a mental note. She poured herself some coffee. She didn't put honey into it, as she would normally have done. For one thing, she wasn't sure about the twirly stick, which was new. The one time she had tried to use it so far, she had ended up with a sticky mess all over the counter. She was really a spoon girl.

"Did you ever read *From Honey to Ashes?*"

"No."

Gloria wondered if this was the right conversation for Day Six. Not that the days had been consecutive. Far from it. That was not what happened in modern life, especially during a pandemic. Building a relationship had to fit in between lockdowns, like everything else. God had gotten five uninterrupted days in on the Creation project before he pulled land animals and humans out of the hat on Day Six. "Yeah," Gloria went on, "It's a book by Claude Lévi-Strauss, a follow-up from his first book about South American myth, *The Raw and the Cooked*. Old now but still cool."

"Hell yeah, old but cool. I'm all about that." Steve nodded, sipping his coffee. She found herself staring at his mouth, at the shapes it made. It was the first time in months she had seen anyone without a mask who wasn't on a screen.

Taking a slow breath, Gloria picked up the thread of her discourse. "Yeah, no kidding. Anyway, in *The Raw and Cooked*— isn't that a great title?—he sets up this opposition between foods that are eaten raw, representing nature, and cooked, representing culture. Then in this second book he talks about honey, which is a food that is processed—prepared, cooked, *cuit*, you know?—by bees, not people. The bees mediate this natural product, nectar; they kind of get out in front of Lévi-Strauss's original distinction and mess it up. Their honey-making is proto-cultural. I've always liked it about old Claude that he didn't just chuck the whole thing right then; he carried on and modified his theory. If honey messed up his category of the natural, then it turns out that tobacco, which you have to burn to ashes in order to use, did the same to his category of the cultural. Culture is supposed to be about fending off destruction: that's what he said first off. But tobacco, you have to destroy it, burn it up in smoke, to use it. Because tobacco was used to communicate with the gods, he theorized that it was kind of post-cultural—at the opposite end of the spectrum where human culture runs out and blends with the divine. Honey and ashes are at opposite ends of a continuum."

"So what happens if you burn honey, then? Which sounds like a great idea to me, by the way."

"I dunno. You end up with some kind of fancy barbecue sauce?"

They had laughed. But the idea had hung on. It had hung on a lot longer than Steve. She didn't much mind. She was usually better off alone. It was just that alone was so much more definitive now. Under COVID, alone really meant *alone*. A society of one.

Burnt honey. That which comes before rendered into that which comes after. Drunk and by herself on New Year's Eve, she actually tried it. To burn it, that is. Not just the cute-ass caramelized honey that you find in recipes. Clear to ashes, that was the idea. Whoosh. As she learned from befuddled googling, pure honey burns very hot. The honey adulterated with sugar—that is, sugar water—tends to self-extinguish, at least in small quantities. It has to be the pure stuff, 18% moisture or less, water-winnowed by bees: that shit burns like oil. Its flash point is 200 degrees Fahrenheit. (She got this from a firefighting website.) With the admirable attention to detail of the inebriated, she set up an experiment over her kitchen sink. By dint of holding a teaspoon of Manuka honey with tongs and then bathing it with flame from an extra-long butane barbecue lighter (Gloria, though an avid barbecuer, was usually afraid of fire) she managed to set it alight. It went up in a terrifying, exhilarating rush and set her single fire alarm off. It made a smoke mark on the ceiling. She dropped the spoon in a panic and ran to her fuse box, illiterately and anciently labelled with faded scraps of tape by some repairman in 1965, flipping switches frantically trying to turn it off before realizing that it probably wasn't hardwired, given that most of her wiring was still knob and tube. Driven nearly insane by the wailing and unable to find anything to climb up on in order to reach the ceiling, she was reduced to smashing the godawful thing with a broom. It went blessedly quiet. She went back to the sink and experienced a revelation.

There was no ash. All the honey had been consumed. The spoon was black and sticky. That was all. Gone. Completely gone. Gloria burst into tears.

There is nothing left between honey and ashes. No. That's not it. You can't get to ashes from honey. Yes. Culture is indispensable. There it is. The physical properties of the universe had just told her something. The fuck. Why do animists know everything? They read the poetry of the world itself, the stuff scientists are just catching up on. Gloria sucked the exceedingly painful blister on her thumb that she'd just noticed. She could put honey on it later.

As her bed spun in gentle circles that night underneath the faded glow-stars on her bedroom ceiling (stars once vitriol green that she had carried from house to house to house since she was fourteen, their color now so tasteful that grownups asked her in all seriousness, where did you get those?) she thought:

> Knob and tube.
> Swish and flick.
> Honey, honey, lion.
> Before the beginning, after the end.
> Knob and tube.

Among baroque variations of these, she passed out.

Spring, the mint grew. Mint is one of those herbs that keeps people in northern climates from killing themselves. She had confined hers, the mint that had once enveloped her whole tiny garden, to two large buckets that delineated the meager path she had struck out, with great labor, between two lines of supposedly robust, shade-loving perennials, which resembled nineteenth-century schoolchildren with TB. She endeavored to be as strong-minded about this as were the original guardians of such children. She watered them and left them palely loitering. A scraggly shrub that she was unable to uproot she left in one corner. Its spindly branches stuck out toward the young perennials in an admonitory fashion, like some horrid matron out of Roald Dahl. The transplanted mint took off like a rocket, of course. Soon the buckets were shaggy with new growth. Her tabbouleh consumption increased dramatically.

The burn on her thumb was giving her trouble. It wouldn't quite heal. She'd put honey on it that first drunken evening, and then graduated to a variety of other topical applications.

Each one would work for a while, then somehow backslide so that the new, pink skin across the ball of her thumb would fissure again. Then it would continue to get worse until she tried another cream, another approach. She had two video consults with her GP, who prescribed various things in turn to no avail and referred her to a dermatologist whom she could not see for seventeen months. So she went back to honey again. This was a bit of a hippie remedy as far as she was concerned, but it did work better than anything else. The only problem was that she had to use it continuously. If she skipped an application for so much as a day—even when the thumb skin looked perfectly normal, healed—the tissue would get red and angry and begin to weep. It was bizarre. Still, if her thumb was addicted to honey, so be it. There were worse problems to have at the present time, though she did worry about her blood sugar.

Like almost everybody else, Gloria had been trapped at home for eighteen months. Unlike many, she hadn't lost her job. She had a degree in Museology, and unlike many people with such degrees, she actually worked in a museum. In her case, it was the municipal art museum, a gaping barn-like place not unlike an underground parking garage, that shared space with the local symphony. As such it catered to school tours and regional projects and listless symphony-goers before their shows. Still, that was enough to keep it going, unlike similar museums in other towns, which sank under the weight of their own earnestness early in the COVID months, probably never to return. Like and unlike, like and unlike: she mulled over these cross-hatchings in her life as she sat for hours in front of her computer, trying to figure out what to do on her shoestring budget, enduring endless visioning meetings, running virtual events in which seven attendees was a crowd. Often people would begin to sign off before she even got through the land acknowledgment. The miracle of it was that she still liked her house. It had two cells: the big living-room-cum-kitchen at the front and the small bedroom-and-bathroom combination at the back. The cubicles of air that were her cupboards (for linen and kitchen stuff), her closets (for clothes), the shelves of her refrigerator, the hollow drums of her washer and dryer, the hot cube of her oven: these were other cells. She moved her scant belongings around among these cells and they changed their state: dirty/clean, wet/dry, bunched/folded, raw/cooked. Her right thumb made honey prints everywhere. She just kept sponging them off with warm water. It was amazing, the number of places she touched in a day. Touch is a sense we often ignore. Honey made a record of it.

One day, as she contemplated whether or not her museum community was ready to host a show by an Inuit artist who did upsetting things with crucifixes, it occurred to her to ask: had it been sacrilege? The honey fire? Had she been flippant and pissed off some dangerous gods of the Americas, as people did when they wore sugar skull costumes at Halloween? Nervously, she wiped sticky traces off her keyboard. That night, she checked over her whole body in the shower as if self-examining for melanoma to see if there were any more raw places, like her thumb. What if, eventually, the condition spread, and she had to bathe her entire body in honey? Or live in a vat of it, or something? A dreadful flash of squirming white larvae went through her mind. There she had been, thoughtless imperialist, on New Year's Eve. Was she now cursed by the honey gods? She would be eaten by bears. She would be made raw. What would a raw human be like? She would put on clothes; they would unravel. She would speak, and it would come out like an infant's prattle. She would have to stop using her stove and cook over raw flame. Or subsist on a raw food diet. Or would she be pushed to the other end of the spectrum—the burnt end? Is that why her thumb refused to heal? It was forever burnt. She would wake up some morning a shapeless pile of ash. Instead of talking, she would belch flame. Or she would pass entirely beyond the material plane: drifting around bodiless, placeless, furious like the rest of the American gods suffering habitat loss. That might be worst of all. Stuck trying to read the careless smoke of cigarettes and wildfires. Looking for attention or propitiation where there was none. Attention, the food of the gods, for which smoke was a cipher: wavering, easily dispersed, not quite material, not quite not.

She came out of her tiny shower—another cell, now that she thought about it—and towel-dried her short hair, which she had cut herself. It spiked out all over; she looked electrocuted. She felt electrocuted. Cooked. Though, naked, surely she was raw? She remembered that Lévi-Strauss's categorical map had another axis: moist and dry. How had that one worked? The trick with Lévi-Strauss was to think of one thing at a time and try to imagine how binary pairs of ideas might cross over it. It was like flipping switches. Take honey. Honey was a wet food, liquid in itself and usually—in the South American native context—mixed with water when consumed, mostly by drinking. But honey was also foraged in the dry season and associated with solar myth. Wet/dry. Here she was, just out of the shower, the place she went to be transformed from dirty to clean. She went in dirty/dry and came out wet/clean. Out of the shower, but still in the bathroom, the larger cell that contained the shower and was adjacent to it, she dried herself: clean/dry. Her hair dried more slowly than her skin, though: she remained, in that respect, wet/dry. So? What did that mean? Well, it showed that hair was weird stuff. Living/ dead. Intrinsic/extrinsic. Retentive/repellent. No wonder people were so fetishy about it. No wonder she had been almost physically sick when she had had to cut it herself for the first time. Now that she was dry—or her skin was—it was more obvious that she was naked. Was that true? If you see a naked wet person, is it more salient that they are wet or naked? Thinking it over for some time, she came to the conclusion: wet. Funny. We think nakedness is so spectacularly noticeable; it's a sex thing. But really, if you think about a nude wet child, an elderly person, a person in the prime of life just stepping out of the shower with dripping hair, what's important? They are all wet; they look vulnerable. Wet people are somehow at risk: risk of cold, risk of drowning, air-breathing animals perilously breaching another element. Think of all those generations of Europeans mortally afraid of bathing. Once a human is safely dry, it becomes naked: then it needs clothes. She needed clothes. She put on her bathrobe. Was she now clothed? Not really. Does a bathrobe count as clothes? In a bathrobe, you are often still wet: damp skin, damp hair. You put it on to cover your dampness, while you wait to be fully dry, or contemplate your choice of real clothes. Clothed/ unclothed, that's the state she was in. An appropriate state for the bathroom, that shower-adjacent space, a space where the more refined transformations from nature to culture take place: where people shave, put on their makeup, adjust their bodies at the skin level. Then they exit the bathroom and put on their public-facing clothes. Frankly, there was no need for her to do that just now. There was no public. She could stay in her bathrobe all day. In that liminal state. Obviously, this was why everyone was so crazy now: they were neither raw nor cooked. Bathrobe-brained. All this explained that annoying thing that people only ever do in movies, when in some state of acute distress they step into the shower fully clothed. It's doubtful that anyone in human history has actually done this, but it is perfectly clear as a mythological statement. Such a person is in a perverse state, for the moment resisting the cultural imperative that clothes exist in order to keep you dry. No doubt this is why swimwear is kinky. She gave her spiky hair another rub with the towel; even damp, it seemed lighter than before, a bit blonder, perhaps from being out in the garden. She left the bathroom: wet/dry, clothed/unclothed, employed/unemployed…

Stray mint plants cropped up around the foundations of her house. She assumed she had not managed to pull up all the root systems. She grubbed up each one like you do with dandelions, scraping her knuckles raw on the cement of the foundation to make sure she got every scrap of underground life. Mint plants, somehow, began to invade her neat lines of euonymus and hosta and astilbe. A young bleeding heart was strangled by a rope-like strand of root that seemed to have sprung up overnight. Served her right for buying something with such a pathetic name, she thought as she pulled the broken and shriveled thing up ruefully and then wrestled the root out of the ground. All the time she was working she had to resist the urge to turn around and peer at the mint lurking in the buckets. How it could have escaped its containers was a mystery. But she was an amateur: the vegetable world is full of mystery. Rooted/spreading. Still/moving. Time-lapse photography had made such doublings almost hideously clear. A few seconds of footage she had once seen of a sunflower turning its face towards the sun in a dreadful parody of sentience had stuck in her head for years. She went in to wash the tingling menthol off her hands at the kitchen sink. Her knuckles were barked from the struggle. Mint had got into them, and they burned painfully. Honey took care of it.

In the dead of night a mint monster crept out of the left-hand tub in her yard, shaggy and rustling, child-sized, with ropey limbs of stem and root, dripping saw-toothed leaves. She saw a nightmare face peering through her kitchen window, head turning slowly this way and that; cones of pink-white bloom protruded into wavering stalk-like eyes around which tiny bees buzzed like dark tears. Moments later, looking out the window pane to the right, towards the skinny sentinel of the single shrub, she saw the creature's small, tense figure, its back bowed in a terrible effort, thin arms and searching fingers reaching down and under her house as if trying to lift it up by main force. It looked like a toddler trying to shift a boulder. You've got to be kidding, she thought. But the mint monster looked very serious. Her house was simply in the way. Plants are really bloodyminded, she thought. Then, presumably, she woke up. She was standing in her kitchen. She must have zoned out or dozed off. Isolation was wreaking havoc with her circadian rhythms.

She checked both buckets, and the mint was undisturbed, growing ebulliently. *Mentha canadensis*. Ubiquitous. Harmless. But definitely raw. And, she now felt clearly, repressed. Would you like to live in a bucket? When it was your natural state to spread out *ad infinitum*? *Mentha canadensis* was the name of the plant in Canada; in America, it was American wild mint;

in China, it was Chinese mint; in Japan, Japanese mint; in Russia, Sakhalin mint. Mint, citizen of the world, crammed into a tub in her back yard. When would the revolution come?

The garden was shaded by tall buildings, but still, there were flowers, so bees came. She was happy about that. Wasps and hornets also began to show up, about which she was less pleased. Bald-faced hornets, in particular; they were scary. Bee-killers, apparently. By mid-summer they were swooping on her threateningly every time she ventured out. She smelled of honey. It was embarrassing to be bossed around by something so small, but she ended up fleeing most of the time. She repressed her shrieks as best she could for the sake of her neighbors. Everybody was tense under pandemic conditions—and everybody was always at home. By-laws that people barely remembered were being enforced. The application of laws at least reminded you of the existence of other people, even if you barely saw them. Gloria searched everywhere for wasp nests in the hope of calling an exterminator, but found none. She began to feel under siege. Maybe she should take up indoor pursuits. Buy a piano. It would look good in the front room and keep her busy for at least a decade. She looked at some ads for second-hand pianos on Kijiji, but held off. She liked her garden.

After a bit more frustrated googling, she ordered one of those fake nests like hanging paper lanterns. When it came, she found it utterly unconvincing. Dubiously, she hung it on a branch of her solitary corner shrub. Within days, the hornets gave up. She could go out safely. It was strange to think that such aggressive creatures could be fooled by such a simple stratagem. Now she was free to set up her one folding deck chair on the tiny flat area nearest the house, where she had put five irregular flagstones that she had bought on sale at Home Depot down on a shallow bed of sand and gravel. This was known, she had been delighted to learn, as *crazy paving*. There she sat, the stones wobbling slightly under her feet, her hair bleaching ever more gold in the sun, and read the slightly musty copy of *From Honey to Ashes* she had found and bought after a considerable online search. Fastidious about her books, she couldn't keep it in the house in case it spread mildew. Instead, she kept it in two ziplock bags, one inside the other, under the chair. She imagined anxious pairs of binoculars trained on this suspicious package from the windows of the surrounding high rises, wondering what kind of drugs were in it.

One evening at dusk, she was carrying dishes to the sink. When she looked out the kitchen window, she saw that the fake nest was glowing. It gave her an instant chill, even though it wasn't some evil spectral greenish glow, but a pleasant warm amber. She dropped the dishes into the water and ran outside. Had her neighbors swapped it out for an Ikea lantern without telling her? Did the thing have some weird solar aspect that she hadn't noticed on the packaging? What the hell? She took it off the shrub and examined it. There was nothing, no hidden battery or solar cell, no filament, no diode. For a moment, as she held it, a warm light with no visible center spilled out from the middle, glowing through the translucent plastic sides. It gave off no heat. The glow slowly faded as she held the nest. When she hung it back up on the shrub, it warmed up again and hung there smoldering like a tiny beacon. Moths began to gather around it. She was completely freaked out. Who could she possibly ask about this? Was the fake nest radioactive? It wasn't like she kept a Geiger counter to hand. Maybe it had been treated with some phosphorescent stuff. But it hadn't glowed before. Bioluminescence? But it wasn't alive. Trembling slightly, she went in.

She did not bring the nest in with her. It might explode. Perhaps it would set off some chain reaction with her electric lights. God knew, it could be some as-yet-undiscovered energy. Isolatium. Photons were in a frenzy about something. Dark matter. Aliens. The old gods. Well, if it were any of those things it could just bloody well sit in her lawn chair and read Lévi-Strauss. By its own light. No way it was coming in here.

Frenzied googling yielded nothing except that the brand she had bought had no light-emitting features whatsoever. She went to the window: the thing was still glowing cheerily, comfortably, as if part of her homey garden design. The wraiths of moths could be seen blundering around it. What was going on? Her 1950s suburban bungalow was located over a ley line? Some kind of micro-incidence of sheet lightning? She had accidentally grown a magic shrub, which was channeling chthonic power up through its branches and making the nest into a lightbulb? She didn't even know what kind of shrub it was.

It was a tamarack, the shrub. It could grow into a tall tree. Its leaves and bark were medicinal, particularly useful for the respiratory tract. It was the only native conifer that dropped its needles in the fall. It was not known, umm, to be light-bearing?

Yet light-bearing it was. Gloria found three empty jam jars, rigged up little harnesses with string, and hung them on the spindly tamarack. Retreating into the house for safety, she watched in the crepuscular light as they gradually, tactfully, lit up as if trying not to scare her. The nest illuminated, too, pleasantly honey-yellow. She stared bug-eyed out the window for twenty minutes, trying to decide what to do. Call the city, see if there was a freak underground cable? Perhaps there was a local elder who could do a cleansing ceremony with sweet grass or something? A priest? A paranormal investigator? The idea of breaking quarantine for any of these was not attractive. She had been so careful so far. Except for that one time with Steve, months ago, not a soul had crossed her threshold for a year and a half.

Perhaps the nest itself was the problem. If she took it off the shrub, though, wouldn't the hornets come back? She'd be trapped inside again. She couldn't risk it. She ordered another one and gave the original to her neighbor, saying that it might help him keep the hornets off, there was clearly a nest around. Mystified, he accepted it and hung it up in his yard. It didn't glow. On her side of the fence, her jam jars continued to light up at night, as if filled with invisible fireflies. When her new artificial nest arrived, same brand as before, with no light-emitting features, it, too, glowed. Moreover, it did not even wait to get to the tamarack, but began emitting soft light in her hands as soon as she got outside into her yard. Ah, going for a light-up model instead? said her neighbor, peering through the slats of the fence. Gloria nodded, bewildered. She didn't know him well enough to discuss the possibility that her yard was full of sacred energies.

Her online reading got steadily weirder, but no practical solution presented itself. As time went on, she began to wonder if hers was a problem susceptible of solution. Did it even need solving? Her hair, usually an unexciting mousy brown, continued to lighten, gradually converging on the honey blond she had been as a child. Maybe she was living backwards in time like Merlin. She did not like this idea. Childhood, then adolescence, young adulthood, these had all been hard enough the first time. She had no desire to live through them again. But then, natural bleaching from the sun was much more likely. This would not explain her eyes, though; she had a creepy feeling that they were yellowing, too, hazel taking on more amber tints, like the eyes of a big cat. This was, of course, impossible. Unless there was some kind of jaundice that only affected the iris, not the sclera?

She tried to quit honey. She ceased eating it and putting it on her skin. Within a week her thumb was raw to bleeding and her knuckles were dry and swollen and beginning to crack. She also—and this was the truly damning part of it—began to feel strangely uncomfortable in her house. Her little bungalow, which she loved: she didn't feel at home in it. It felt cold and sterile. She missed the smell of honey on the walls and surfaces. The transforming power of all its subsidiary cells—the washer, the dryer, the shower, the stove—felt less marvelous than before, more quotidian. She held on for twelve days and then resumed her honey habit. Everything improved again.

Lévi-Strauss's tale variations on *The Girl Mad for Honey*—a title with which she was beginning eerily to identify—usually resolved once the girl had made the right marriage. These were usually to birds: to Woodpecker, say, who was an excellent honey-hunter. A number of problems with this approach occurred to her mind. Her life lacked the scale, fluidity, and decision of myth. Nor did it revolve around the elementary structures of kinship. She had parents, and one brother; she hadn't seen them over the pandemic and wasn't worried about it. Her relations with them were ho-hum. Her father had been military; the family had moved constantly as she was growing up, with the result that she had known a lot of people in a lot of places and remained close to none of them. Far more absorbed with coping with the endless parade of new schools and peers, neither she nor her brother were well-bonded to their seemingly indifferent parents, despite sharing houses with them in many diverse and sometimes stressful places across the world. The one thing she had learned over the fifteen-year period until her father's retirement was that she liked old things. Old things held their value. She'd been to plenty of museums and resolved to train in Museology.

So, marriage was off the board as a solution. She was not the marrying kind. She was about as likely to marry a bird as a man, when she thought about it. She looked speculatively at the Woodpecker—he was, admittedly, a fine specimen—who came to tap on her windowsill but made no overtures.

She booked the Inuit artist with the transgressive crucifixes into the museum. It was time people faced up to things. She had a very awkward conversation with the office of the Diocese of Huron about it but went ahead regardless. There was a social media furor that involved a grand total of twenty-seven people. The gallery was pleased, as was the artist. The tamarack in her yard began to turn yellow and drop its needles. This was natural. What was not natural, she had to admit, were her eyes: they were now, unquestionably, amber, like those of a cougar. If and when she ever went back to the office (which possibility seemed increasingly unreal) she would have to claim that she was wearing colored lenses. People would probably put it down to some internet kink she had gotten into during the pandemic. The nest, and its accompanying constellation of jam jars—she had not been able to resist adding a few more, hung on the tree and ranged about its thin roots—still glowed snugly in their places every night, honey yellow. Nights came earlier, and darker, so they were all the more spectacular. Feeling that she might as well accept the *status quo*, she had taken to pouring libations of honey water at the foot of the tree every now and again. Ants appreciated it. In myths it was often important to keep ants on your side. Their gratitude was useful. Once she looked out to find a raccoon licking the ground with concentrated thoroughness, as if grooming or pacifying the earth after a wound. The sight was comforting.

Mint isn't evergreen, but it is tough as hell. It was still hanging on in its buckets at the end of September, riding out the first frosts, unwithered. Flying bugs were dead; there was no more danger of hornets. Gloria could have put away the fake nest, but she couldn't possibly take it down. What was it that Ursula Le Guin had said, in some later novel? *You must not refuse the blessing.* Then, on the night of September 22, she was once again doing dishes. She was looking out the window absently, a dish cloth hanging from her hand. (A dish cloth. Wet, it performed the transformation dirty/clean. Dry, it brought wet things into dryness. It was a magnificent instrument of culture, a dish cloth.) The autumn evening was dark. The lights glowed on the tamarack. She saw a brief, flailing shadow against their radiance. It wasn't a moth. It was bigger. It was thin and ropey. Snaky, almost. Knobs and tubes. Gradually, unbelievingly, she made it out: it was the mint monster, dancing. Spidery, thin-limbed, gnome-like, ropes of stem and jagged leaf twined into two legs, two arms, a twiggy torso, a long neck and a tiny head with a ruff of leaves along the top like a bird's crest. It was wiggling and jerking its frail limbs manically, whirling them out from the center with half, and sometimes complete, rotations. Its object was the yellow glow of the nest, a captured sun surrounded by jam-jar stars. Gloria felt a huge horror-movie scream building up inside her, but after a moment it dwindled away.

She was gripped instead by pathos: at the tininess, toughness, desperation of the twig-like creature; at the calm luminescence of the lit globes. This was an end-of-season event. In it was expressed the strange and tireless life of plants: it seemed to her that it was the mint's last hurrah to an enigmatic light before it succumbed to the die-back of winter's darkness. What else could it be? Surely any light was the sun to a vegetable intelligence? What does a plant do when it encounters the sun? It moves toward it. It moves before it. It moves because of it. It moves. In the mint monster's wild capering was an entire season of movement, a recapitulation of its relationship to the sun from May to September. She thought back to its heroic effort to lift up her house, its tiny bowed back straining: inexorable, unreflecting, strong. The time would come when the mint would win. For a millisecond, it came to her in a dizzying flash, the millenarian perspective of mint: her house, that stupid lump, that big stone, that bucket, eventually it would be gone. Redeveloped. Bombed. Abandoned. Mint would creep through the foundations; it would pull itself forward on its belly, root and leaf, root and leaf, through the hole where her house once had been; it would get to the other side. She felt an upwelling of awe.

The mint monster threw back its crested head. It flailed its whiplike limbs. Implacably, the light in the nest and the jars shone. We make of the world what we must, *mutatis mutandis*. That which needs changing having been changed. She and the mint had both been changed by the immanent power that was operating here, the *genio terrae*, backyard deity, whatever it was. If this was the mint's response, it was eloquent. She could think of nothing so expressive in her own life. Unless, perhaps, she considered as she began to dry the dishes again, she was now enacting her daily transformations—wet/dry, bunched/folded, unpeeled/peeled—in a ritual spirit. Certainly they seemed somehow larger and more solemn than before, as if surrounded by a halo of empty space. Though this could just be an effect of the echo chamber that was the pandemic. Still, it seemed small potatoes next to the mint's magnificent recapitulation of its own being. *Small potatoes?* Hmm. Was she being *vegetablist?*

She watched the mint monster dancing for a long time. She did not record it on her phone or post it online or any of that. She watched it attentively, admiring its restless energy. At midnight, it still showed no signs of stopping. She went to bed, leaving it to its solar worship, or whatever its minty business was.

When she awoke, it was cold. She went out to the garden. There had been a hard frost: the mint was withered and blackened in its buckets, as if burned. Dead/alive. Mint was a perennial, she reassured herself. Still, tears rose in her eyes and spilled over. Elton John's aching chorus rose terribly in her mind: *hold me closer, tiny dancer…* She tried to pull herself together, thinking sternly, no, of course not, it's not like that. I don't hold the mint and the mint doesn't hold me. We lead parallel lives. The lines never meet. Not really. Then she thought of the weird little scrabbling creature trying to throw her house over its shoulder, and broke down again. The tears were hot in her amber eyes, cold on her cheeks under her yellow hair.

Autumn progressed. High winds stripped the trees. The lambent nest, which she had tied on with string for safety, remained on the tamarack. She took off the jars, thinking that they would crack in the cold. This possibility seemed disrespectful. The integrity of vessels was important. Vessels made the difference between inside and outside. Her house was a vessel. She was a vessel. She didn't want those to crack, did she? Just so.

Like most of the rest of the world, Gloria stayed home and kept working remotely. COVID was still raging. She and her three colleagues tried to come up with innovative digital programming. Their efforts were about as lame as everybody else's, tired images and processes that barely covered the alternating rows of zeroes and ones that constituted them. Something/nothing. She endured a bit of chaff over her new eyes and hair. Ha, ha, funky pandemic look, who knew blondness was a side effect of COVID, at least it wasn't weight gain, that was such a drag, and so on. Speech/silence.

She read the rest of Lévi-Strauss. There was a lot of it. Her mind grew full of frogs and capybaras, macaws and jaguars, tortoises, opossums. Stories of the origins of water and fire. The necessity of wearing feathered penis sheaths. Many words that described appropriate states of exogamy. She learned that honey bees, *apis mellifera*—the *white man's fly*—came to the New World with the European colonizers. All pollination across the enormous continent had previously been carried out by native species, stingless bees of many varieties, as well as wasps. So the bees that environmentalists wailed about, the desperately important bees that pollinated all the crops in the Americas, they were neither native nor wild, but feral, like mustangs. They were not, in the strictest sense, natural at all, but cultural, products of domestication. This fact was unsettling. It turned a certain amount of environmental rhetoric on its ear. Culture, in this case, wasn't encroaching on nature. It was encroaching on previous culture, culture piling on culture. The diverse population of native pollinators was gone by the nineteenth century, along with most of the human cultures that had told stories about them. And all those peoples, the ones called native, the supposed wild humans of the American continent, they were feral, too. All humans were feral. They escaped from Africa, if we think of that as the cradle of human culture. They escaped from Eurasia, if we think of that as its crucible. They walked into the Americas over land bridges and glaciers, walked west and south, bringing with them that pattern of domestication and escape, domestication and escape that is human migration. Stop/start. Tame/wild. *Langue/ parole*. Humans, ever evasive, ever inventive, the ultimate invasive species.

Winter came on. Snow fell early. She struggled to clear the sidewalk in front of the bungalow within twenty-four hours of any snowfall, to the bare cement, as the by-law said, even though almost nobody went by because the children at the nearby school were all online. The law was the law; it held back chaos. She shoveled snow. She avoided the use of salt to spare the environment. Remember Carthage? She got away from her computer screen. Resentful/grateful. The two lines of pared-back perennials in the garden stood in arrested development, nubbins under the snow, quiet and blank. They looked cold. They looked overly regimented, as if marshalled in front of a firing squad. Or like soldiers enduring a long harangue in Russia somewhere. She wanted to bring them out cigarettes. The wooden half-barrels with their neat vertical slats and iron rings looked like jails or ammunition silos. Mint, she knew, was plotting within them. Nights, the amber light of the nest washed over the desolation in mild reproof.

New Year's was slowly approaching, the anniversary of her honey/ash experiment. The whole idea of an anniversary was troubled: then/now. Once/recurring. What was she going to do?

She was going to do it again, of course. What a question. Rituals are made to be repeated. She looked into her honey eyes in the bathroom mirror as she hand-cropped her tattered honey hair. She mulled over the fizzing contents of her skull, burbling like fermenting mead, old/new, old/new, old/new. Culture. That's what it was. A process. To the person who learned even a bit of it, it was new, no matter how ancient it was. Interacting with a raw consciousness, the sugar and water that were the perquisites of organic life, culture, like a wild yeast or a kombucha SCOBY, even in the tiniest traces, changed its host. Things bubbled up. *Mutatis mutandis*. She had not realized how ready for a change she was.

Advent crept by, day by day, on soft paws.

She decorated the house in white and gold for the holidays, just for herself. Most people who decorate do so for their own pleasure. For the shock: familiar/strange, ordinary/festive. She made long garlands of popcorn to feed to squirrels and birds in spring. She tucked small sprays of cedar and yew, plucked from local hedges, into corners, over doors. Enter/

exit. Hello/goodbye. She chose all the gold glass balls from her carefully stored packages of Christmas decorations. She only ever bought glass ones. She was a purist. She put them in bowls on every surface and lit candles near them at dusk. Tea lights and white emergency candles: at two heights, they doubled the flaming reflections in the glittering orbs. She played Orthodox Christmas music, solemn deep amber chants and golden kontakions that seemed to coil up slowly from the gathered tongues of fire. She would have burned incense, but she knew from long experience that she was allergic to it.

She felt like the high priest of something, but she wasn't sure what. A priest, though, she thought, as she clicked her butane lighter and dipped its flame into the well of a tea light, represents a community. She watched the tiny bead of flame. She imagined the mint monster's crested head turning toward it. As she moved around the room, click click click, igniting more candles, she pictured its crazy little form twirling from light to light giddily, drunk on photons. As mint was dormant in winter, like the ants and the bees and many other creatures with whom she shared her property, maybe she was their priest, a stalking primate still moving around in midwinter, making celebratory fire. Keeping the sun indoors, like a tame animal. A dangerous pursuit, indeed.

Nights were clear and cold now, with little snow. The light in her yard burned, clear gold and unconsumed, among the LEDs and electric strings that adorned her neighborhood. Some people, she knew, were breaking quarantine to have people over. Six people, eight people, family groups, bubbles. Venturing into stores for shopping. She still had everything delivered. The government was issuing advisories and holiday guidelines. Folks were going through nasal swabs like they were going out of style. She invited no one. No one invited her. The pandemic had brought out a truth she had always known: she had no friends. In her experience, friends were overrated. She did not miss them, any more than she did her family. She cooked a guinea fowl with all the trimmings on Christmas Day and bought a huge bag of nuts in the shell, which she scattered in the yard for all comers: squirrels, raccoons, jays, cardinals. The little garden was a riot of color and noise; she served up the golden bird, gazing at it hungrily with her golden eyes as she devoured it like a bird of prey. Eaten/eater. She felt a bit guilty about the mint, trapped in the cold and dark: perhaps a bit of compost?

December 31st, 11:45 PM. Second New Year's Eve of the pandemic. This time, she disconnected the fire alarm. She didn't need a mechanical chorus. She felt that she had a living one: a head full of capybaras and bright macaws, a yard full of slinking, scurrying, or nesting creatures. Inside/outside. Perhaps she could even speak for Woodpecker, with his golden eyes. She finished her last glass of champagne, unhurried. At three minutes to midnight, she began. Tiny tongues of flame from her butane lighter licked the edges of a glistening spoonful of honey, its reflection weirdly bent in the curvature of the metal basin. Floomph, the honey went up. It cried to heaven. Rawcookedburnt. Offered/denied. Sweet/acrid. Alone/together.

She dropped the spoon, clang, a blackened clapper, into the hollow inverted bell of her sink.

She turned. Something walked into the room. Sun Honey Bee Lion. Bright gold. *Gloria*. She felt sweet breath. *Gloria*.

The God That Got Away

*Deus absconditu*s, that's what they said. It's colossally unfair. I did not abscond. Moreover, with that verb there's always a hint of impropriety. The chimney sweep absconded with the poker. The vicar absconded with the silver. What I am supposed to have absconded with? People's belief? So I'm a belief thief now? I suppose so. If I've departed and they're still believing. It is the business of gods to propagate belief and to be the objects of belief. This is the name of the game. The purpose of a god is to be believed in. This seems like a fairly low threshold, but it is surprisingly hard to sustain over the long term. And if, as Luther and Pascal and so on would have it, the god who absconded in the sixteenth century was the only one remaining and was therefore in principle the necessary object of everyone's belief, presumably that universal belief departed with said god as a kind of attachment. Belief, I'd like to think, would tend to inhere in a god. Yet at the same time, of course, perversely, it must also remain with the believers, for how else would they be believers? Being thus in two places at once, I suppose belief must be described as an entanglement. This may be the kind of thing that is easier to explain in German, which uses the same verb for *to borrow* and *to lend*.

The terrible stretch of this belief between two points unimaginably distant from one another apparently constitutes the productive tension of Protestantism. They've all been twanging like bowstrings ever since, to great effect. It's a quantum approach to the problem of salvation. On this evidence, I can certainly concede that it was time for me to abscond.

But I didn't. I really didn't. Let us consider it rationally. First off, there is a problem of reference. It has never been clear to me that I am the god to which so many theologians—including, for the sake of argument, Luther—and sacred scriptures refer. This is a tremendous amount of information, all in all, and almost none of it applies to me. The guarantor of rules. The dispenser of arbitrary grace. No. This is all utterly peripheral. But—and this is the key point—there does not seem to be anyone else available to whom it might apply. There's just no one. Only me. I obtain. Where, exactly, do I obtain? Now this is tricky. Let us say, everywhere. I admit this is rather an appalling claim. Everywhere. Right through you, and your neighbor, and your father and your dog and Napoleon and Sappho and the Large Hadron Collider and nitrous oxide and T-Rex and rhododendron leaves and microplastics and all space and time. It's a lot to take in, I will say. But then, I don't have to take it in: it is in. Me. Everything. As far as I can ascertain, there does not appear to be the tiniest particle of anything that is not part of the system that is myself. Precisely what this means for the status of other consciousnesses I cannot determine. But as these seem also to obtain, I conclude that each must just look after itself. That would seem to be the point of having a nice hollow skull full of yourself while still being in the midst of me.

Trained reasoners will have spotted the related problem. If I am everywhere, there is nowhere else for me to go. Nowhere to abscond *to*. In short, I am right where I have always been— or at least as far back as this, my consciousness, extends, which feels to me illimitable—which is to say, ubiquitous. Omnipresent. Existent. It is better to exist than not to exist. Anselm was onto something there, in the *Proslogion*. Yet I cannot imagine not existing. Can anyone? It is, perhaps, a similar problem to the one we were just considering: like looking for the other side of everywhere. It does not obtain. Whatever kind of being it is that I am, I am all about existence. Indeed, I am a complete catalogue of all existents.

It has occurred to me that perhaps I am not a god at all, given the foregoing. Belief has no obvious agency in this picture. I persist in being, seemingly, despite the misbelief or unbelief of all the millions of people on Earth who believe in a god and who might attach that status to me, however inaccurately. What kind of god is sustained by erroneous belief? By belief so wide of the mark? It makes me doubt the whole premise of godhood. Or more particularly to ask if, in the end, I might be exempt from that status. Alternately, we would have to reformulate what it means to be a god, and I for one feel that my current definition really gets down to the nitty-gritty.

So. There remains the matter of immanence. This is a cherished concept for me, and one that offers solutions to several of these conundrums. It cuts right through the Gordian knot of reference, for one thing. It is not really possible to refer—to point toward—something that is immanent, as it has (like me!) no fixed locus. It cannot be distinguished from anything else, being everywhere. You see the beauty of this? I find it quite edifying. Incidentally, the idea of immanence also offers all these hapless theologians an out: instead of being hubristically wrong about nearly all aspects of divinity, they are grappling with a failure of categorizability. Of course, it is impossible to talk about the ineffable. That goes without saying. I go without saying. I carry on endlessly, invisibly operating—invisible, that is, *in toto*, as there is nowhere external from which to gain a perspective. Humans, you know, have their eyes stuck in the front of their heads and must unendingly look at something. It is sadly limiting. I do not share this limitation and have no practical difficulty with being everywhere all at once. I feel no compulsion to believe in myself, being satisfactorily filled up with facts. I love facts. I am, you might say, the sum total of all facts. It's the scale of this proposition that boggles people's minds, I suppose. Poor mites, I can hardly blame them. Aha, but yes, then there is immanence. Surely this is what I have been describing all along. How I am distributed through all things, which things are fully present as themselves, but also as me. It's not that I get in the way of things; more that I am the way of things. Glibness crops up all too easily in discussing this state of affairs—my apologies. I am beginning to think that I should self-identify as a monad. Loneliness, though, in such a state must be a factor. Is there, perhaps, a monad support group?

This brings me to my final point. My complaint. It is amazing how much communication in general tends toward complaint. I speak, of course, of the unfounded accusation that I am the *deus absconditus*. I insist that this is not so. It is not possible for a universal deity—which is what the monotheists we have mentioned all posit—to abscond. Think about it. Luther was fond of claiming that the *deus* of the Old Testament was very hands-on; he was physically present, chatting on the front stoop with Abraham, burning bushes and so on, whereas in the New Testament the deity is far removed, dwelling in majesty in the remote sky, letting the great automaton of Earth tick over of itself. I myself do not recall any such events, nor any commensurate distinction in my way of being. I conclude that if they happened at all, I was not involved. Nor, as I have said, have I been able to identify a being who might have been, anywhere or at any time. It is theoretically possible, I concede—and it's an exciting, though alarming, possibility— that such a being might exist, absent from everywhere, one who did actually succeed in absconding. As such a being is unthinkable to me, I can obviously say no more about it. My predicament, though, is different. The whole absconding business strikes me as cover for a human shortfall in the perception of immanence, one that is unfortunately increasing in prevalence. I fail to see how this can be my fault.

The whole notion of creation as being my responsibility— or, at any rate, of its belonging to the *deus absconditus*—is also one that rings no bells of recognition with me. I don't recall creating human beings, or indeed any other beings. (Perhaps I did, and perhaps those memories were eclipsed, and that was the moment I absconded?) Making, being made: I don't really feel them as part of my purview. The system that is me is self-organizing. It requires no input from me, or at least no input of which I am aware. Being. Being is my thing. Yes. Just being in being. I don't mean to sound petty—after all, I am huge—but it seems to me there has been a real falling-off in mystical apperception lately. The feeling of the self as a percipient; the exactness of the things and their interrelations in space and time that are the objects of perception—the Rose window of the cathedral hovering in blackness, the crispy thud of brick stacking on brick, the glorious arc of someone jumping a skateboard up the curb—these are no longer commanding attention the way they once did. There's a general shortage of epiphanies. People aren't looking at the world, or if they do, there's not enough inside them to set up any cosmic reverberations. Thus I am invisible. I mean, I have always been unseeable *in toto* due to the scale problem, but now I *feel* invisible. I experience it as a deprivation. I have only ever been recognized in details. If those go unperceived, what's left for me? Of me? Perhaps this is the belief that I rely on, if I am, after all, a god. Immanence deserves eminence, does it not? So, many theological doctrines would suggest, but then, they are mixed up with so much nonsense that it is difficult to rely on them. Still, I feel alone. Unseen. I don't remember feeling this before. There's a great deal of me to be alone. Is aloneness relative? Is a really big thing more lonely than a small one? Or am I experiencing some kind of knock-on effect, as all the constituent parts within me feel more alone? There has definitely been a loss of interior harmony: ecosystems are coming undone; parts of the whole are acting alone. Maybe I am being affected by sweeping violence and sadness interiorly. I am an immanent being with an auto-immune disorder. Who can cure me? Who? In order for a cure to be effected, it is first necessary for the doctor to notice the patient.

I am patient. I am still here. I promise you, I never did abscond. Help me.

The Hand of M. R. James

I think it will be seen, from what has been
said, that my subject is one which depends for
its actuality upon the accumulation of a great
number of small facts. There is, of course, a broad
historical background: no less than the whole
history of Western Europe since the period of
the Barbarian invasions.

—M. R. James, *The Wanderings and
Homes of Manuscripts* (1919)

It wasn't until she put in her application for full professor, in
the first year of the COVID-19 pandemic, that Helena realized that the neatly penciled notes she had read in grad school
accompanying this or that manuscript had been written by M.
R. James, the famous ghost story writer. This was twenty-five
years after she'd left Cambridge herself. Nobody had ever discussed the other life of the famous codicologist as an author of
weird fiction. Likely it was embarrassing. Still, she suspected
that someone must have at least mentioned it at some time,
as she had a cat named Montague. It's a good name for a cat.
Montague. Never Monty.

Who could possibly have mentioned it? She had been surrounded by medievalists and had certainly had no inkling then
that anyone who taught her read twentieth-century fiction,

not even such turn-of-the-century productions as those of M. R. James. The likeliest candidate was the dapper, Dickensian fellow who had taught paleography, James's own discipline. It was the kind of out-of-the-way fact, drawn from everyday life, that he might have dropped in. He was better adjusted than most. He was even married. It was not impossible to imagine him experimenting with antiquarian Gothic fiction in his off hours. Reading anything approaching to horror, or anything closer to horror than hagiography, seemed beyond most of the other personalities she could recall: the spectral linguist whom she had observed actually wringing his long, pale hands at meetings; the spiky heresy expert, who resembled nothing more than a praying mantis in a glossy, dark wig; the rake, who lived in his own private, but very compelling, eighteenth century. Horror had been likely to overtake the latter, but retirement had fortunately intervened. On the other hand, while house-sitting for a couple of famous philologists, Helena had been impressed by their collection of mysteries, mostly of a cozy, vintage character. Whodunnits have a standing appeal to a certain kind of medievalist, this being precisely the thing that it is nearly impossible to determine in manuscript culture.

James, though a manuscript expert, had never written a whodunnit in his life. He was the other kind of medievalist, Helena thought. The pessimist. The manuscripts he had spent his life working on were largely anonymous, their existence and their preservation alike the products of nebulous, impersonal forces. Worthless items were collected; precious ones evidently lost. The pressures of history, of style, of occasional bursts of charisma were to be felt, almost palpated, in the corpora of writings he described and catalogued; they were rarely explicitly revealed. His fiction had a similar character. It was never whodunnit, but *what's* done it. What implacable, untraceable entity has gone and scared the living hell out of some hapless, learned person? Why is it that being able to anatomize the cathedral with great exactitude will not save you from the terror that lurks within it? Is it not overwhelmingly likely that being the kind of person who has an eye for a good rood screen has placed you in danger in the first place? Casual readers might not think of James as an ironist—horror is not often thought of as an ironic genre—but that is exactly what he is to a medievalist's eye. Time after time his nerdy narrators are overtaken by precisely those entropic energies that they contend with professionally. They are haunted by the ghosts of their own erudition. The medievalist in modernity: that is the horror of M. R. James.

⌫

Montague—the cat—was doing the best of the family under conditions of social isolation. There was greater competition for beds and chairs, but beyond this he was unconcerned. He usually won these competitions, anyway. Sooner or later someone would get up to pee or snack and return to find him curled like an apostrophe in whatever warm place he or she had left. Cats prevail. Helena's two teenage children and her husband Phil, also an academic, were variously stressed. They all saw a lot more of each other than they were used to. Everyone did more cooking. Novels, video game campaigns, and long-back-burnered research projects were intermittently undertaken and abandoned. As the late spring came on, volunteer tomatoes, beans, and kale sprang up in the garden beds. Both parents looked on this with relief, as garden centers were closed. Neither had liked to picture the wasteland of the summer without the vegetable patch. Packaged seeds, and even seedlings, could be ordered online, but this option was somehow horribly attenuated: how could such vegetables thrive, flattened and deracinated by online commerce? Neither of them were believers in the internet of things. They preferred to cultivate such sports and genetic survivors as sprang up naturally. They all knew: their family was one of the lucky ones. Nobody worked in service or ran a small business. These had been decimated within weeks of the outbreak. They had no elderly relatives in care. Many of these were dead. Terrible news poured into the household from all media channels, but aside from eczema from the constant hand washing, and a generalized anxiety, they were surprisingly, blessedly untouched. Helena and Phil made donations to the local food bank and began to prep their online classes for the autumn term.

Helena, having always been as blind as a bat, had had expensive eye surgery two years previously. Results had been terrific for about eighteen months—waking up as a sighted being, able to read the clock radio or go swimming without goggles—but then had begun to pall. Her new implanted lenses, which she had naturally assumed would be immune to cataracts because they were made of plastic, began to develop swimmy, blurry spots. It turned out that the high tech multi-focals for which her natural lenses had been swapped out were still contained within natural integuments: these were developing spots of opacity, mini-cataracts. Being a cyborg was not what it was cracked up to be. She was seriously out of pocket and her vision was nearly as bad as it had been before, except now neither glasses nor contacts could help. There was a laser procedure available to address the problem, but clinics were all closed because of the pandemic. It was maddening. A two-minute zap with a laser would restore her sight. Drugstore reading glasses were a pretty inadequate solution. While this certainly counted as a first-world problem, Helena had to repress occasional flashes of dread. It was a serious impairment. She did spend most of her professional life reading. There was a lot of stuff she needed to look at that could not be transposed onto her iPad and blown up enormously.

Her eyesight changed from day to day as the spots swam around. Weird floaters intermittently crawled across her vision. The most bizarre effect of all was that from time to time she began to see printed words, clear as day, inside her closed eyelids. This began to happen after she had spent many hours working with text, magnified as it now had to be, on her backlit screen. Alcohol drastically enhanced this effect. Standing in the kitchen preparing dinner during those awkward hours that the French have sensibly written off to drinking—*cinq-à-sept*—became surreal. Every blink would be accompanied by a graven black phrase hanging in front of her eyes—*Did the Khazars, or a significant portion of the Khazars, headed by their king, convert to Judaism or not?*—while her open eyes looked at carrots or watched her hands open tins of tomato purée. Lying in bed at night after a bottle of wine and a movie, a neat paragraph would hover in the air above her as if projected onto the ceiling, surrounded by a haze of orange-yellow light. She found that she could even make these paragraphs scroll. Her mind's eye could contain about five lines, reminiscent of the ancient Mac, with its nine-inch screen, on which she had written her PhD thesis.

In an effort to combat the floating print problem, she took to writing notes in longhand. Not all the time, but regularly enough to give her eyes a break. It had been nearly two decades since she had written anything by hand except grocery lists.

She was out of practice. Years ago, as an undergraduate, she had been proud of her handwriting. While it was not a perfect cursive like her mother's had been—the kind that had once been taught in school—it at least counted as joined-up writing. She had spent a lot of her money on crappy fountain pens, and her hands had been constantly ink-stained, a bluestocking effect she had secretly admired. Now her efforts looked scraggly and thin. Perhaps it was time to invest in another fountain pen, a grown-up one this time. Maybe a Waterman.

⚔

During this phase she also became addicted to audiobooks. This came as a shock. She despised actors and the ways actors read books. Still, by judicious sampling, she found a good selection of books that she could stand hearing aloud. These were mostly long English and Russian novels of the nineteenth century. Naturalistic fiction was a bit of a gap in her education. She preferred British readers who did not speak through their noses. As a break between monumental efforts like *Middlemarch* or *The Brothers Karamazov* she listened to Sherlock Holmes stories and turn-of-the-century popular fiction on YouTube. This was how she had discovered—or rediscovered?—the work of M. R. James. It was a relief to find protagonists to whose unusual knowledge she could relate. The state of the Book of Common Prayer in 1653 or the aftermarket in topographical mezzotints were a lot more intrinsically interesting to her than the different varieties of cigarette ash or how much bruising could be sustained by a corpse after death.

Helena, although she very much enjoyed the atmosphere of bohemian bachelor London that Conan Doyle created, eventually got tired of the simpleminded hubris of Holmes. The problem was a professional one, she decided: Conan

Doyle had been a doctor who despised medical practice and had failed in it. Holmes was compensatory, therefore: treating his clients like patients, forensically investigating crime as if it were disease, the great Sherlock was a doctor *manqué*, a clinician with a terrible bedside manner who nonetheless effected cures in the criminally afflicted. Crime is simpler than medicine. Holmes was thus able to succeed where Conan Doyle had not. Any Victorian doctor would necessarily have spent his life surrounded by frustration and enigma; the profession at large was steeped in unscientific old habits, error, ignorance, and malpractice. All of this disappears at a stroke when Holmes becomes a *consulting detective*, a specialist in crime, that range of curable illnesses in the social body. In this respect Holmes's treatment of Moriarty was nothing more than a dilation and curettage. Holmes, as an addict, was a physician unable to cure himself, but that was as far as insoluble problems went in his world. That was why the Holmes stories were comforting; they were good stories to fall asleep to. James's stories, on the other hand, were good stories to stay awake to: enigmatical, they were excellent companions in insomnia. Shy and misanthropic gentleman experts though they were, like Holmes, James's various antiquarian protagonists stayed true to the anxiogenic conditions in which they spent their professional lives: their adventures were unresolved, inconclusive, partial, dark. It wasn't that they spent their lives in dank Gothic castles or dimly illuminated libraries—most libraries, you will find, provide good lighting—but rather that it really is the job of a manuscript scholar to face the unknown, day after day, hour after hour.

Helena was desultorily putting together an article on Middle English wonder tales about Central Asia. This was rather at the edges of her expertise, but then, it is the point of expertise that it should be clear about its own limits while sniffing and scuffling around enthusiastically on contiguous terrain. This process meant that she had an accumulating set of handwritten notes in a large coil-back Hilroy exercise book that she had unearthed in her study. She had been delighted to find this relic of her previous life, and every time she flipped through its pages of intercalating headings, notes, and queries she remembered the words of her Grade Six geography teacher: "I want to see your work in a notebook. One that you can't put pages into or take them out of." This had been the best advice of her school career. Single sheets of paper get lost. You will never have the discipline to organize them into binders. More importantly, writing things down in the order in which they come to you, and being able to trace what that order was, reveals how non-linear thinking is. The process of thinking something through is messy and recursive. It is full of interruptions and tangents and lines and squiggles. It forces you to invent private hieroglyphics so as to impose degrees of order. The fiercely idiotic templates that her children were expected to use to construct essays in school gave her the heebie-jeebies for exactly this reason. Such templates went a long way to explaining why first-year students in her classes were wholly unable to think. Of course, her children simply wrote their essays and then went back and filled in the stupid boxes afterward. They were only stymied when the essays themselves were obviated, and just the templates were required, as was increasingly the case.

Helena was charmed to find that certain of her own personal tics, little marks and signs that she had not seen for years, instantly began to populate her new handwritten notes. They were perhaps even more noticeable than they might have been because they were almost twice the size they would normally be: she had to write really big to see anything. It was like being a neophyte: her abstruse notes looked like they had been written by somebody in primary school. One of these private signs that really took her back and made her feel positively nostalgic was an arrow with a jagged lightning-bolt shaft. This arrow, appearing regularly on the left margin of the page, meant, at its simplest, "I am talking now," and marked an interjection. She had evolved it while taking lecture notes when she wanted to distinguish what the professor had said and what she thought about it. It was so useful she soon began to use it in article and chapter summaries. Its range of meaning moved flexibly from "now, what does that make me think of?" to "No!" to "this idiot doesn't know what he's talking about." It was invaluable.

Helena watched this jagged arrow recur in her notes about Prester John and Tengrism and Rubruck's travelogue and thought comically that it was her mantic sign. Admitting to having a mantic sign and going so far as to obey it were the only things she had ever liked about Socrates: it was his one point of simple deference to mystery. In listening to his mantic sign, he had been like any other Greek, accepting oracles. In her case, whatever it was that followed the jagged arrow often had an oracular quality. Frequently they were questions. Such questions could pertain to matters quite far from those apparently in hand. Or they were partially recalled quotations or disparate facts from other domains of knowledge, suddenly parachuted in. They were epiphanic. That much she had always known. It had always been part of her process. If she had ever wanted to get to the heart of a research topic, or find the thing that a paper was going to be about, all she had needed to do was follow the track of the lightning-bolt arrows. Thinking about it now, she probably should have put one at the beginning of her full professor application. *Zap. Jagged arrow. I am talking now. Here is the mystery that is me.*

⌒━◦

One day, re-reading her notes about the vexed question of the Judaism of the Khazars, she noticed one particular jagged arrow and its following remark. She could not remember writing it, though the same could safely be said about all the rest of her summary of the particular article she had been reading. This is why we write summaries down. The line read:

> *The whole thing gave the impression that it was the work of an amateur.*

Its relation to the cultures of the Asian steppe was not obvious. Nor was it a fair comment on the article in question, which was competent. She must have been in a bitchy mood. Some pages later, amid some notes on Icelandic romances set in medieval Russia, she found:

> *Few people can resist the temptation to try a little amateur research in a department quite outside their own, if only for the satisfaction of showing how successful they would have been had they only taken it up seriously.*

It was true that her Old Norse was marginal. Her husband's was much better. Finally, a lightning-bolt arrow in her notes on Ahmad ibn Fadlan's account of his travels among the Bulgars said:

> *I expect that with you it's a case of live and learn.*

If this was her mantic sign, it was a lot more mantic than usual. She could not recognize the voice at all. It did not read like one of her own interjections. Yet the idea that somebody could be gaslighting her via notes for an article on Middle English wonder tales was ludicrous. In her own hand? In a bound notebook to which sheets—thank you, Mr. Edwards of Sixth Grade geography—could neither be added nor taken away? It wasn't like they had been composed in some hip collaborative forum. Nobody wants to collaborate with anybody online about Middle English. It wasn't a glitch in the matrix. It was more of a locked-room mystery.

She suspected her husband. He was locked in the same house with her 24/7, and he could read Middle English. From him a jibe about her amateurism in Old Norse far-traveler tales would be fair comment. But that was ridiculous. Why would he bother? She asked him about it. She showed him the notes. He pointed out that he had seen plenty of weird shit in her notes over the years and went out to water the tomatoes. "It's just the voices in your head," he said, kissing her forehead. "Don't worry about it. I love those voices."

She examined the coil-back binding of the exercise book. It appeared intact. She reviewed the writing. It looked like her own, or like the current iteration of her own in its more straggling form. She had no examples of her former style, as all her notebooks from grad school and her early teaching life were locked in her office on campus, and she couldn't get to them. She had never had a curly, girly hand in particular, but somehow she remembered her previous specimens as a bit more rounded. These were scratchy and upright, more donnish to her eye. But that may simply have been the lack of the exaggerated curves made by a wide-nib pen. So much for material traces. What did that leave? Self-hypnosis? Maybe she could Skype with a medium who could advise on the parameters of automatic writing? She googled the intrusive texts.

They were all from stories by M. R. James.

Why Helena's self-doubt would take on this particular avatar was an open question. Her promotion brief was still pending. It seemed to her that this aberration was a marker of professional stress. M. R. James, she assumed, would certainly not have approved her full professorship. She was a woman and a colonial. Her brand of literary criticism would have been unrecognizable to him: not scholarship at all. He hadn't even been a full professor himself. Provost of King's College, Director of the Fitzwilliam Museum, but not a full professor.

Her brief would be pending for a year. Was she going to spend twelve months putting up with snide remarks from an old-school codicologist? He would be impossible to please. Opportunities to exercise the kind of expertise he had once had were rare in Canada. Even rarer now that no one could travel to foreign libraries. Instead of articles on Middle English, perhaps she should take up writing porn. James had been notoriously fastidious. If her notes became suddenly graphic, he would surely go away. But then, porn was ghastly and bored her to death. Its omnipresence was one of those things she simply could not understand, like Twitter.

After all, she told herself soothingly, all professional women run into horrible old men who seek to wound them at one time or another. It's just that these men are usually still living. To be entertaining the censure of a colleague who had died in 1936 seemed unusual. On the other hand, if it were actually possible, it would be ubiquitous. In the sciences, there was an ever-growing list of women who were and are excluded from patents and prizes; in the humanities, where there are fewer patents and prizes, maybe the equivalent was this kind of beyond-the-grave hazing. Should she ask her female colleagues about it? Had any of them been harassed by dead men in their fields when they sought promotion? Could it be grieved?

⚬══►

She carried on assembling her notes. The materials were diverse and interesting. Certain stories cropped up again and again in various guises. A persistent one was Shopping For A Religion. The *Primary Chronicle* of Kievan Rus had their leader, Vladimir, upon deciding that it was no longer accept-able to be pagan for reasons of trade, convene a meeting of representatives from the three major monotheisms: Judaism, Christianity, and Islam. A priest from each faith spoke his piece. Vladimir rejected Islam out of hand because of its taboo against drinking, was unimpressed with Judaism, as the Jews had lost their capital of Jerusalem, and reserved judgment on Christianity. He then sent out emissaries to examine the faiths of the region *in situ*. Orthodox and Roman Christianity were the two major contenders, and Orthodoxy won hands down as soon as the Rus got one look at Hagia Sophia and its splendid ritual. That was that. Vladimir married a Greek princess and had everyone in his city forcibly baptized in the Dnieper—man, woman and child—upon pain of death. A different vari-ation was available to explain the religion of Khazaria. This powerful Khaganate had been, at least mythically, run by Jews. An oft-repeated story of the eleventh century had an originary leader of this empire, Bulan, convene a similar meeting. Un-able to decide between the three options, he cannily asked the proponent of Islam which of his two rival religions would be more acceptable to him. The man replied Judaism. Bulan then asked the Christian which of his two rival religions would be more acceptable. He likewise said Judaism. The king and his courtiers accordingly adopted the Jewish religion, though they continued to preside ecumenically over a multi-faith population, particularly in their great, and now lost, city of Itil. Helena had yet to find a version of this debate tale in which the ruler declared for Islam, possibly because that religion had been so overwhelmingly successful throughout the region that it needed no apologists. Only the Mongol invasions of the thirteenth century had caused a bit of a rollback. Genghis Khan, who knew that he was well on the way to becoming a god himself, was unmoved by proselytizing monotheists. However, in his vast empire he tolerated them all, in addition to Tengrists and Buddhists of several stripes. The sheer scale of the cultural activity on the central Asian steppe—the numbers of people, languages, and religions involved, the timescale and the distances people migrated—made the European history of the period to which she was accustomed look very, very small. There was a certain comedy in being concerned about what a couple of insular chuckleheads in York and London thought about it all.

Amateur, repeated M. R. James. Jagged arrow.

Helena felt that she was obliged to accept this zinger from a man who had been able to compare the Greek and Ethiopic versions of the *Book of Baruch* while still in elementary school. How had the fourteen-year-old James ever hit upon Baruch? He had, apparently, translated it from Amharic while still at Eton. A couple of lines from Baruch were included in the Anglican Christmas liturgy. Perhaps that was it. Christmas had always been a crucial time for the mature James, the point in the year at which he would trot out his latest ghost stories for a small fireside audience at King's College. Dickens had started that vogue, of course, replacing the primary haunting of the season—the one of which Mary had been informed at the Annunciation—with a safer one. What ghost is more terrible than the Holy Ghost?

Meanwhile, the news got worse. The murder of a black man by a policeman in Minneapolis caused a wave of protests across the United States. Hundreds of thousands of people, defying whatever protocols their local governments had managed to set up in the face of the apathy and denial of the central administration, surged together, breathing one another's air and fury. Scenes of apocalyptic unreason swept through the media. A plague makes some things clear. If the poor and disenfranchised are dying anyway, why should they not meet on the barricades? What have they got to lose? They are already the walking dead. Still, watching them walk and scream and rage, only to be crushed by police armed like zombie hunters, was horrific. A communicable disease shows us all too plainly the truth that crowds of people are toxic to each other. Stress levels rose in Helena's household. Not so much with her, as she had long since learned to live in a near-total media blackout and saw little of it, but the kids were jittery. Searches on COVID-19 symptoms rose appreciably. Tabs were opened on Spanish flu, cholera, and Ebola. A few on structural racism and rioting. Helena insisted that the family watch *Les Misérables*.

She began to write an initial draft of her article, which meant composing more onscreen. It was simply too slow in longhand. The floating-print problem cropped up again. She would lie awake at night with one of her more lackluster sentences—the one she had stared at longest in order to cut or revise—floating above her face at a distance of about three feet like something out of a horror movie. *There is a long-standing debate in historiography about the extent to which premodern people believed their histories to be fact, and how far fact is understood to be from story.* The words would hang there tidily, in Times New Roman, from twenty to forty minutes until something or other happened to her optic nerve and they would fade away.

One night at around 1 AM, after a day in which family distraughtness had generally been high and Helena felt sure that both kids were still lying bug-eyed in their beds with their Ear-Pods in, the following sentence appeared as she closed her eyes:

> *Awake he remained, in any case, long enough to fancy (as I am afraid I often do myself under such conditions) that he was the victim of all manner of fatal disorders: he would lie counting the beats of his heart, convinced that it was going to stop work every moment, and would entertain grave suspicions of his lungs, brain, liver, etc.—*

She had not read this sentence on her backlit screen that day. It hung there, wavering slightly in a taunting manner. She was certain it was James. After a moment, as it refused to go away, she turned the light on and looked up the text. It was from "Oh, Whistle and I'll Come To You, My Lad," a story in which there is a certain amount of sinister insomnia. As she scrolled through the story on Project Gutenberg—indeed, just as she found the sentence in question—it occurred to her, with a genuine thrill of horror, that she had never actually *seen* that sentence before. She had only *heard* it as an audiobook recording. For some reason this realization was appalling. It emphasized the craziness of the whole business. Entire bodily systems were being hijacked. They were being cross-wired. M. R. James, in her head! Is there insane synesthesia?

When she turned the light off and lay back down, trying to pretend she was calm, only a fragment of the utterance was left, hanging in the dark:

(as I am afraid I often do myself under such conditions)

⚬━⚬

The next morning she checked her browser history to make sure she had not *read* any M. R. James. She hadn't. She had none in print. She had heard the stories read aloud. Her visionless brain had set them in the air in Times New Roman. She tried to picture herself explaining this in an online chat to her GP. It did not seem to merit breaking quarantine and trying to get into the office or trying to admit herself through emergency. Hospitals were crammed. M. R. James was not urging her to self-harm or to harm others. Disapproving of her application for promotion, if that's what it was, surely counted as non-urgent. Gaslighting, of course, is regularly taken to be non-urgent: that is why it works. But then, his most recent communication might be construed as one of solidarity.

She talked it over with her husband. He agreed it was weird but said that it was just her unique way of coping with lockdown, promotion anxiety, and headlines full of imminent doom. "M. R. James, eh? Haven't thought about him in years. If I ever have. Just think of him as a remote higher-up scrutinizing your application. The provost, say. Someone you'll never even meet."

Helena's provost was a Caribbean economist named Ramkalawan. She was not sure that M. R. James would feel that he and this man were necessarily on the same side. This thought was rather liberating, considering that the provost actually existed.

She went on drafting. What else was there to do? Who wants to do online yoga?

M. R. James, it turned out, was a complicated man. There was Helena in her kitchen at 6 PM, compounding jerk marinade. She had the recipe for this as a single sheet of A4, copied out of an ancient library book in her husband's spidery writing, which she had tucked, years ago, into her paperback copy of an excellent old book called *Traditional Jamaican Cookery*. Despite the excellence of the book, her husband's recipe was better. Public library cookbooks were one of the main reasons the two of them had survived grad school, both in terms of relief reading and the accumulation of practical kitchen skills. As her eyes watched greenish-brown sludge whirling in the food processor, she saw superimposed over it at every blink:

> *It is a very common thing, in my experience, to find papers shut up in old books; but one of the rarest things to come across any such that are at all interesting.*

Helena, who could cook dishes from three continents and a wide variety of outlying islands very creditably, experienced a flash of irritation. Shut up, James, you old snob! But then, how much cooking had he ever done? In this line, his expertise had probably been confined to making toast.

She spent the next day struggling with the critical framing of her essay. This was always an exhausting process, like trying to fix the interpretative locus of a needle in a haystack.

Retiring early with the headache that too much critical theory always gave her, she received, flickering like old film footage before her closed eyes, the following gruff concession:

> *I didn't like to confess that this was beyond me.*

So, was this about the food or the critical theory? Imagining M. R. James eating, much less cooking, spicy jerk chicken was pure comedy. Picturing him trying to navigate the fearsome ideologies of present-day literary study verged on the pathetic. It would be about as successful as her attempt to translate *The Book of Baruch*. This short sentence dissolved unusually quickly. She was left lying in the dark with her head pounding. She would frankly have welcomed another remark or two, just for the distraction.

⚔

Listening one afternoon to "The Tractate Middoth," which was clearly set in the Cambridge University Library, well before the open stacks or (primitive) computer catalogue of her day, suddenly recalled to her a story that she used to tell when drunk at cross-grained colonial parties during her PhD. It had actually happened to her in the Reading Room of the UL. This was a large and patrician room filled with long tables and reference books. Among the wide selection of books available there for people to seek out and pull off the shelves for themselves was the complete run of the *Patrologia Latina*. This took up two mid-length shelves in one quadrant of the room. On the opposite side of these shelves were the *Patrologia Graeca* volumes, which she never had any occasion to consult, as she knew no Greek. She did not like to imagine what might have happened to her had she ever ventured to that side of the shelf. Her encounter with the Latin Fathers had been sufficiently damning. One afternoon she had had need of some book or other from the series that lay about midway along the shelf. The aisle between the *Patrologia* and whatever benighted Latin patristic sources lay opposite to it was quite narrow. It was tricky for two people to pass one another, should they ever need to (which was, even in those days, not often). She was making her way along toward the middle, when suddenly, with lightning speed, a little old man in a drab suit with a toothbrush moustache was there before her. Blocking her way with his tiny form, he proceeded to look high up on the shelf and low down on the shelf and left and right along it. With a Canadian politeness at which she was absolutely infuriated and yet could not repress, she had had to stand there for fully ten minutes while he deliberately and with great ingenuity prevented her access to these monuments of masculine wisdom. His eyes gleamed with silent malice. She had stood there fuming, wondering if perhaps she ought to volunteer to lift him up to some of the higher volumes, as it was well within her capacity and certainly not his, until he made a feint and retreated a few steps. Able to move along toward her goal, she was just stretching out her hand toward the volume in question when he snatched it and scuttled, crablike, away. This evil sprite of the *Patrologia Latina* was, in her opinion, entirely the equal of the desiccated, cobwebbed, and extremely dead clergyman who had haunted the Hebrew stacks accompanied by a dreadful smell of must in James's story. God knows, it had probably been the same man.

There is no prescribed place for this, so far as I know came up, rather primly, in the notes she had resumed taking not long after, as soon as she had re-told the tale to her husband, who snorted reminiscently. Could this be an apology? It sounded conciliatory. Did James disapprove of such misogynistic rudeness? And further, did this imply that he had *overheard* her? She had not included the library anecdote in her notes. She had merely spoken it aloud to Phil. This increase in James's ambit was worrying. Had he been hanging around in some ghostly fashion as she played the recording of "The Tractate Middoth"?

When she retired to her bed that night, to her surprise, she was abruptly confronted behind her eyelids by the stentorian tag:

QUIS EST ISTE QUI UENIT?

This made her giggle. The use of Latin in any kind of horror is funny. But she could not help thinking that this was exactly what had been running through the mind of the man with the toothbrush moustache, as he had watched her progress up the *Patrologia* aisle. *Who is this who comes?* The fact that women had not been allowed into the University Library until 1854 was actually a central point in the dénouement of "The Tractate Middoth."

Was M. R. James making a joke? Sharing a joke with her? A Latin joke?

The capital letters faded quickly and were replaced. Hanging there jauntily in their stead was:

> *Now, years ago, I took great pains to learn the Latin language, and on many occasions I have found it most useful, whatever you may see to the contrary in the newspaper: but seldom or never have I found it more useful than now.*

Helena thought of J. K. Rowling, earner of the highest-grossing Classics degree of all time. Not one of James's Old Etonians had even come close to her, despite their looting of India. Did he know that? Had he, perhaps, read Harry Potter through her eyes? (*Tolle, lege!*) She tried vainly to remember if she had re-read any of the series since her promotion brief had been submitted. Rowling aside, however, it was certainly Helena's facility in Latin and other antiquarian subjects that had secured her a stable university job, for which she had especial reason to be presently thankful. Her job was secure, and it was one that could be done in a meaningful way remotely. Surely we can say that a medievalist always works remotely? Her scientist friends were going mad. Scientists need labs and extraordinary numbers of machines and flunkies to do anything. They can't accomplish much alone. The letters faded slowly from her inner sight, with *great pains* hanging on the longest, like the smile of the Cheshire Cat.

⊂══⋊⋅

By July it was hot. Enormous storm systems rolled over southern Ontario like steam trains. The temperature was regularly over 30 degrees. There were tornado warnings. A hailstorm flattened half the tomatoes. Humidity was so high that having to wear masks in public was a serious trial. People were seen carrying them by hand, limp and soggy, and snapping them on five seconds before ducking into the air conditioning of the pharmacy or grocery store. Some people gave up on masks entirely. There was more general chafing, complaint, and denial about COVID-19 restrictions. These had been eased but were by no means gone. Stir-crazy toddlers and preschoolers, deprived of play parks and splash pads, drove their parents wild at home. Older kids, now that the last of their feeble online classes had petered out, had even more time on their hands. Options for summer jobs or camps or sports were minimal to non-existent. The internet seethed with pornographic rage. A lot of the work force was still out of work, savings were spent, and many people who had been doing okay, getting by, six months ago were now desperate. The government was pouring out relief money like water.

Universities set up student assistance funds. Helena paid into one, and Phil another. He had taken up learning a whole lot of tricky new Chopin, and when the timings got too maddening, he would flee outside and trim something savagely with shears. She was at the time-frittering, footnoting stage of the article, a phase with which she had never been patient. Thunder rolled continuously, and there was night after night of sheet lightning. The cool, damp, candle-lit atmosphere of M. R. James's tales became a sensory relief. At night, Helena lay naked under a ceiling fan going full tilt with brackets and colons flashing before her weary eyes, listening to stories set in Viborg and Felixstowe, where cold sea winds were always blowing. After a certain point, wondering about James's unusual silence, it occurred to her that female nudity was likely to keep him away indefinitely. She was not sure how she felt about this. It was hard not to sympathize with a man who wrote tales in which two men who lived together in the country were automatically suspected of necromancy. Yet there were others in which men lying innocently in bed were attacked by hairy, toothed vaginas and had to retire, trembling, to wake all night in another room fearing a fate worse than death. There was a persistent association of women with spiders.

As she faffed around with the expiring corpse of her essay—the final edit was something she always thought of as akin to embalming, the general smoothing-down and tucking-in and rendering unexceptionable—and the plague-stricken world at large reeled apocalyptically forward, new waves of the disease striking all the time, James remained persistently silent. It occurred to Helena that he had lived through the Spanish flu epidemic of 1918. She wondered how many people he knew had died in it. Not to mention all the patrician boys from Eton and Cambridge, his students, who had perished horribly in the war. And upon his death in 1936 the world had been rousing itself, fitfully and gruesomely, for World War II. "Oh, Whistle and I'll Come To You, My Lad." If he was reading the news along with her, perhaps he just did not want to go through it all again. Hauntings may be said to move in both directions. Who says the ghosts are having fun?

Helena got rid of her article. She sent it off to the editorial board of *Reticulum,* and it became their problem. There it would languish for the next year or so, seeking peer review and provisional acceptance and the inevitable revisions required by the anonymous readers consisting of citations of particular works that, of course, were their own, followed by line-editing, the painful making-up of abstracts and keywords for online databases, and finally, publication. This could be counted on two to three years after submission. Helena had once unwisely complained about this pace to a colleague in media studies, whose research domain was confined to a moveable twenty-minute window and been told with cheerful dismissal that after all, Middle English wasn't going anywhere, was it?

Would this be the end of her spectral correspondence with M. R. James? She had no other immediate research plan in view, and it did not seem probable that he would linger in order to comment on her domestic life, even though her promotion brief was still pending. She wouldn't be writing any more notes for a while. She had contemplated starting a journal, but she wasn't the journaling type. She always found other people's lives more interesting than her own. She had false-started on a number of journals over the years but they had always withered away. She would watch people in cafés scribbling indefatigably in mock leather notebooks and wonder what on earth they were saying. Her daughter filled volumes of them, about which she had no curiosity whatsoever. Her only other option would be to take up golf, which, judging from its prevalence in his fiction, must have been the other passion in the life of James. This was about as likely as belly-dancing. She loathed golf. Plus, golf courses across the globe were still closed. Though, she supposed, they were among the likeliest of all sporting venues to re-open soon, as capable of accommodating social distancing quite easily. Golf has always been about social distancing.

⚬══◦

As she folded a stack of towels some days later—a large stack, as her appeals to her teenage children to use them more than once usually fell on deaf ears—she reflected that throughout the *oeuvre* of M. R. James there is a pervasive fear of laundry. (It is, of course, doubtful that James ever did any of his own laundry.) The story for which he is probably most famous, "Oh, Whistle and I'll Come To You, My Lad," features a set of bed sheets that become horribly animated; in other stories there is a wide array of creepy draperies. There's a set of self-rustling curtains that spawn a creeping creature composed out of dry hair; in the numerous walking or crawling figures of horror that he invents, there's considerable emphasis on their cowls, cloaks, capes, and other flowing garments. Academic gowns, by which he would have been continually surrounded, must have given him some anxiety. What was that about? Had he glimpsed Something Horrid in the Hamper as a child? But then, the ability to see the uncanny in the everyday is the mark of the weird fiction writer generally. There are no exotic locations in James, no alien landscapes; his protagonists are usually going about their scholarly business in places no more picaresque than East Anglia. Into uptight, arid lives, inexplicable terrors intrude, sometimes fatally, often just enough to unsettle all certitudes. They come with a dry rustle, the kind of sound you might hear in a library. Moths beating, pages turning. Nothing squelchy or tentacular for M. R. James. As she thought about all this, Helena found that the slight friction noises emitted by the towels as their terry fibers rubbed across one another gave her a certain *frisson*. *Frisson* and *friction* are, after all, etymologically related. She considered various comedy monsters her family had made up: the sock monster, for example, who lurked in the basement, stealing and eating single socks, or the *cussikin*, a tiny creature formed of lint, who farmed and ate dust balls in the same locality. They seemed less funny and more threatening than they had before, when they had featured in bedtime stories.

The scrabbling of squirrels inside the house walls, to which she had formerly been resigned, began to wake her up at night. Domestic flies, unavoidable in summer, began to freak her out. They reminded her of a hellish plague of flies in a particular James story. She traveled the house with a fly swatter. All in all, she was tense.

> *It was now that something happened of which I can certainly not yet see the import fully.*

Such was the bulletin she received from M. R. James inside her waking eyelids on the morning of the day she received an apologetic form letter from her old Cambridge college about their handling of an inquiry into complaints of assault and sexual misconduct, one that was rapidly becoming a scandal in the British press. James, former Vice-Chancellor of Cambridge, evidently remained attuned to the problems of its public image even from beyond the grave.

Helena was accustomed to throwing out or deleting all communications from her old college unread. They were simply dressed-up demands for money that she had no intention of giving them in a world of far more deserving and needy parties. It was remarkable that she had even glanced at this one. It was as if she had been primed by James's earlier enigmatic statement. She thought wryly that she could pretty well guess James's sentiments on this topic. And sure enough, all she had to do was close her eyes some minutes later to read the expostulation:

> *The examination of these records demanded a very considerable expenditure of time.*

Helena was angry. Her inner monologue for the rest of the day was full of brutal remarks to or about M. R. James. She read everything she could find about the college crisis. She read a number of classic feminist essays for James's edification and several Wikipedia articles about rape culture. No doubt it was all news to him, she fumed inwardly. She went to bed drunk and cranky, and soon received the following communiqué, haloed in orange light:

> *It is to be supposed that he made himself very agreeable to the servants, for within ten days of his coming they were almost falling over each other in their efforts to oblige him. At the same time, Mrs. Ashton was rather put to it to find new maidservants; for there were several changes, and some of the families in the town from which she had been accustomed to draw seemed to have no one available. She was forced to go further afield than was usual.*

This was singularly unhelpful. It was hatefully irrelevant. Helena sat up and did some ireful googling and checking of texts in Project Gutenberg. The results brought her temper up short. The eerie paragraph was from the story "The Thin Ghost," which concerns a patrician boy named Saul, a plausible and well-bred young man being looked after by clueless and self-satisfied guardians. He proves to be a necromancer, performing weird rites and raising the local dead. And, as the paragraph still flickering before her eyes at each blink made ironically clear, he had also been a domestic predator: abusing the servants and, particularly, the maidservants. So. The cold fate meted out to him in the story had been, among other things, the punishment of a rapist, one harbored in an educated and elite household that had turned a blind eye to what he was doing. Here was James, once again, finding the horrific in the commonplace. The paragraph hung there blandly for the usual forty minutes or so and then faded away. Helena felt chastened. It occurred to her to wonder, for the first time, if this whole hallucinatory business with M. R. James was a two-way street. Had she managed, in her brief program of feminist reading, to change his mind? Is it possible for the recalcitrant dead to be re-educated?

Helena's eyesight continued to deteriorate. It was alarming, as well as exceedingly frustrating. She wasn't quite fifty and had the visual acuity of an eighty-year-old with dual cataracts. The interrelated facts that she had brought this on herself by going in for voluntary surgery for no better reason than vanity, and that in normal circumstances it could all be cleared up in a two-minute burst from a laser, haunted her constantly. She had to give up showering because the all-white interior of the shower became terminally confusing and she couldn't navigate the space. She had always preferred baths anyway but was perversely upset about this, raging about it to Phil, who could do nothing but shrug. Or she thought he shrugged. Her children's faces looked like she was peering at them through a pane smeared with Vaseline. Teaching term was coming, and it was becoming increasingly clear to her that she was going to have to ask for some kind of accommodation or reduction of workload. It took her a very long time to read anything on screen, and the little talking heads on Zoom were impossible to see. Never having had to do anything of the kind before, she found it horrifying. One conversation with the occupational health liaison for her faculty about options for using speech software for the visually impaired reduced her to tears. She felt she had maxed out her ability to deal with new software in the general chaos of the online pivot. The stuff was expensive, complicated, and she would only need it for a couple of months until the medical system opened up a bit and she could get into the eye clinic. In the end she opted for a course reduction for one term. The whole thing made her feel inadequate, but for the first time, she was faced by a hard physical limit. She tried to think of this as instructive. After all, it had happened to Milton. In his case, there had been no possibility of amelioration. A brain that had spent most of its time processing text had had to make its own radical adjustment to composing blind. This he had done, of course, magnificently, but in so doing he had used up the goodwill of his daughters—forced to read to him in languages they did not understand due to their own haphazard educations, and to transcribe hours of poetry from dictation by an irascible perfectionist—so that two out of the three of them never forgave him. Milton's daughters, unsung, unpaid, uncredited, had been the equivalent of the zoom function on her iPad or the voice transcription software she had been offered by the occupational therapist. Invisible female labor. Invisible not only to the blind Milton.

She found that she could still cook. She relied a lot on muscle memory and rarely cooked from recipes, anyway. She had no fear of knives. She could watch television, which she still did regularly with Phil in the evenings. TV is so formulaic that she could follow it easily just by sound and blurred images. If anything, it sharpened her appreciation of the soundscape of most shows, which do much more work than she had previously understood. She learned, indeed, of a whole new class of person whose work she had never thought of before: foley artists. Professional noisemakers. They do a lot more for us than we think, if we are consumers of media. She also developed a new admiration for the voice work of actors, both those on television and those she heard on audiobooks. Not having to see them made her like them more. That was something. It was a slight increase in the number of things to like in the world. She took walks in her neighborhood, staying on familiar routes. She noticed smells more, and she noticed the palpable quiet on many streets. People were not driving, not endlessly moving about as usual. It was like the social world had disappeared because she could no longer see it. God knows how many neighbors she offended by walking sightlessly right past them. But this kind of obliviousness had been characteristic of her even when she had had regular eyesight. As she walked, she reflected on the strange phenomenon she was experiencing with the floating texts of M. R. James. These never seemed to afflict her when she was outside, perhaps because of the high light. (She wasn't confident enough to go out in the dark anymore. She couldn't distinguish anything.) It was an indoor, readerly phenomenon. James had been an indoor, readerly man. It seemed proper to his person that she didn't hear his voice. He'd spent his life curating texts; it made sense that he would use snippets of them to communicate. It was a kind of *sortes Biblicae*. She pictured the tweedy James chuckling softly to himself, copying lines from his collected works, a few here, a few there, in his rapid upright hand, onto small slips of paper and then floating them along some stream of inner sight, where she, text-deprived, rose to them like a trout to bait. Was it just a parlor game—the kind of spooky game that might be played at Christmas, James's favorite season for ghost stories—or a more serious form of divination? Second sight? Insight? Compensation for going blind?

⊂≡×⊃

Second sight! What kind of sight might that be? came the sardonic words inside her eyelids as she lay down that night, full of wine and cop shows.

It begins with "there is more in heaven and Earth" appeared after that. This was decidedly snotty. But James had never been one for explanations.

⊂≡×⊃

She was left pondering the heaven and earth remark for a long time. James had seemingly retreated back into whatever parallel universe he usually occupied. With her article done, and not much satisfaction to be gained from extra house cleaning—what is the point if you can't see the result?—Helena was left spinning her wheels. She spent her days shunting between a limited number of domestic spaces: bed, kitchen, couch, elliptical. Elliptical, kitchen, couch, bed. Such was, in the terminology of her teenage son, her *grindset*. Grind suite? *John the miller hath ground small, small, small...*what was it?... *the king's son of heaven shall pay for all.* She didn't think so.

89

Jagged arrow. The peasants' revolt had long since failed. The Apocalypse began twelve thousand years ago, with the Anthropocene. There's no paying that back.

More things in heaven and earth, Horatio, you pedant. Than are dreamt of in your philosophy. Or even your philology? She really didn't want to begin another article. She had a list of possible topics. She always had a list. But there wasn't much incentive. What was she supposed to do with herself? She couldn't wait around indefinitely to hear back from her long-dead colleague. What would he have done, deprived of his libraries? With nothing to catalogue? He would have written more ghost stories, presumably, to add to his annual Christmas hoard. He would have turned to his other self, the one his medievalist colleagues did their best to ignore. She remembered Socrates, that smug little prat, listening to his mantic sign, writing a few lines of poetry while he waited for his hemlock to arrive, just in case he had been pursuing the wrong career all his life. Jagged arrow. She decided to write a story about a medievalist haunted by the hand of M. R. James.

The Pickled Boys

"Timothy, Mark and John,
put your fleshly garments on!"

—Eric Crozier, libretto for
Britten's cantata *Saint Nicola*s, op. 42

5 June, 1948: the opening night of the first Aldeburgh Festival, three years and one month after VE Day. Benjamin Britten's Saint Nicolas cantata is having its première. The war is over, but suffering isn't. Far from it. Saint Nicolas is an important saint to Germans, but to see beyond such boundaries is the job of the British ecumenical imagination. The cantata had actually been commissioned by a prestigious boys' school in Sussex for its centenary, but the school governors, with a commendable desire to support public morale in difficult times, had agreed that its initial performance should be to open the new festival. The governors, indeed, have not yet heard it. None are capable of reading the score. The music master can and has; he has his private reservations but feels unable to voice them because of his reverence for the great Britten—like himself, a pacifist.

Yes, yes, says an august voice in the front pew (the cantata, as sacred music, is being performed in Aldeburgh church)—Christmas commission, you know. For the boys to sing in honor of the day. Feast day of Saint Nicolas, sixth of December. Spirit of the holidays and all that. We'll have to cart in some tenor, I understand, but our lads will do all the rest. First time Britten has ever composed for amateurs. Oh, and we'll need some girls. For atmosphere. Wind and waves and so on, they tell me—a blue-veined hand waves to the female singers in the side galleries—Trust the women to make waves, hey?

It all begins. People are respectfully quiet. It's been such a labor of love and self-sacrifice to bring it off, a festival at this time. Most people are still living on the edge. It's a miracle. A great appeal goes out at the opening: the people of today calling back through time to Saint Nicolas, all the way, as the program helpfully points out in tiny, paper-saving print, to fourth-century Asia Minor, for aid and inspiration. It's all very joyous in a stentorian sort of way, like an old uncle trying to let his hair down after a Christmas brandy or two. Like people stretching their tired, miserable minds back to a time before the war. It's a bit like that. But then, it's hard, too. It's Modernism. Life isn't easy; why should art be easy? Music?

By the time Saint Nicolas has been born and sprung out of the womb crying *God be glorified*—which would be terrifying, ghastly as something out of an old penny dreadful, when you think about it, really—and spent a considerable amount of time maturing by wandering about as a solo tenor, some people are becoming silently restive. They are beginning to peer at the minuscule notes as Saint Nicolas calms the waves of a terrible storm. Then he spends some time in prison. Reading ahead— there aren't all that many words in a cantata, but there's a lot of music—a few people notice what happens in Part Seven. They begin to jog each other's elbows. Nicolas, released from jail, attends a feast at a travelers' inn. He's there with everyone, they're just digging in, raising their forks to their mouths—

To eat the pickled boys. The pickled boys. Three young boys preserved in brine by an evil innkeeper and sold as pork. Saint Nicolas is still singing his last anxious strains from prison as eyebrow after eyebrow is raised, pew after pew, throughout the whole church. There is a completely silent, completely pervasive alarm: part apprehension, part insurrection. *Pickled boys?*

The music master of the school in Sussex bows his head in a kind of holy terror. His fear has come to life. Universal outrage. He had known; it was too *outré*. Cannibalism at Christmas. He is going to lose his place over this, and after he had kept it all through the war. He witnesses wordless, grim nodding between two senior masters in the front row. He knows they are picturing, as he is, the awful pantomime that this is going to become: the school's three youngest singers, sweet-faced sopranos, stuffed as if lifeless into a barrel, then popping out to sing *alleluia*. It's a nightmare. This, their great commission, the school's musical legacy. He covers his face with his hands as the choir begins the tavern scene.

Part Seven, which everyone now awaits with bated breath, begins convivially. But things are not what they seem, as is indicated by the mournful music of some mothers seeking their missing children—this comes sweeping in laterally from the female singers sidelined in the galleries—and Saint Nicolas begins to suspect. This is no ordinary pickled pork. He calls out and stops the company from eating. Fingers stop moving and meat lies inert on their plates, presumably. *Boys*, cries out Saint Nicolas, *boys! Timothy, Luke, and John, put your fleshly garments on!*

The music master, shuddering, keeps his face hidden, for he has been struck by a gale of horrified laughter. He is so very glad that this is not an opera; that there are no props. What travesty would that lead to? He tries not to imagine the glutinous chops on the inn table stirring, rising, forming themselves together into lumpy wholes, glazed eyes rolling, broken mouths opening...

In the cantata, Timothy, Luke, and John arise, miraculously, and sing. A collective breath is released. To the credit of everyone's good taste, there is no guffawing. There is one outburst of sardonic applause. The music master raises his face for an instant. He is fairly certain who it is likely to be: the maths instructor. The man has a macabre sense of humor. Yes, so it is. For a moment he has the crazy urge to join in, to celebrate this spectacular moment of inappropriateness. But he thinks firmly of his job and the necessity of continuing in it. It is nearly a miracle that it has remained secure. He suspects that strings were pulled to keep it so: how he remained in nominal employment despite being, as everyone believed, a loathsome conscientious objector, an able-bodied man not at the front. Years of opprobrium he has endured on that score—and not wrongly, for he had been a conscientious objector. Old men will always despise young men for not taking risks to which they are not subject. So will women. He has, perforce, learned to put up with it. In fact, his war had been quite other. Though it had occurred on English soil, it had been international, involving translations from many languages. He has signed the Official Secrets Act, that great reminder to all British subjects that they had best keep their mouths shut on many topics.

The church doors open. As Saint Nicolas is going from strength to strength in acts of holiness and building up towards his glorious Christian death, not everybody notices. The music master, still peering between his fingers at the maths professor, catches a glimpse out of the corner of his eye.

Three pale, shambling figures are making their way up the aisle. They are very small. Children. Naked. They walk slowly, uncertainly but inexorably, toward the altar. The cantata, in its final peroration, collapses in on itself. Whispering begins, then screaming.

The children, two boys and a girl, are variously mutilated. The boys have been cut apart, their legs and arms disjointed. Seemingly, they have been sewn back together, or patched; raised red seams run across their thin bodies. The girl is whole, but the skin across her back above her wasted buttocks is rucked up and wrinkled; it appears she has been partially flayed. All their eyes are dull, their faces hollow; they move with a grim determination, as if called. *Put your fleshly garments on!* A chemical smell—formaldehyde? vinegar?—wafts from them as they move haltingly past the audience trapped in the pews, jostling, pushing, falling over each other, trying to get away. There is chaos now. Saint Nicolas is forgotten. Men and women are running toward the exit, dropping a litter of shoes, bags, canes, handkerchiefs.

The children are halfway up the aisle. The church now resembles a half-empty beach with the tide running: detritus everywhere and only a few people, either paralyzed with fright or beating a hasty retreat. No authority has mustered itself to act. The priest has fainted, so no help is coming on the ecclesiastical side. The famous tenor and the conductor have placed themselves, arms spread, in front of the trembling choristers remaining on the dais, as if saving them from unspeakable assault. An infant screams blue murder in the arms of a belated young mother struggling to extricate herself from a jetsam-blocked pew, intent on saving both her child and her only pair of stockings. A tall, gaunt woman in a navy suit that still has a military air about it eyes her with contemptuous sympathy but cannot go to her aid. She is taking the pulse of the elderly man seated next to her, who appears to have died of fright. Once a headmistress and now a headmistress again, she had been an ambulance driver during the war. She has a pretty good idea who these children are. She is also an amateur hagiographer. So she alone knows that Saint Nicolas, in addition to saving the pickled boys, saved three young women, from a family made destitute, from being sold into prostitution. Britten's librettist had not mentioned this for reasons, she reflects ironically, of decorum. She lets go the old man's neck. He is clearly dead. He may be counted as the last casualty of the war. As she rises to go to the young woman's assistance, she thinks of what might have been had that story been included in tonight's cantata: of the hundreds of thousands of women, resurrected from degrading deaths, or lost in the twilight of enduring shame, pressing into the church, listless, desperate, filling it up completely, spilling out through the doors, clambering on each other's shoulders, uncountable. Mercifully, Britten's Saint Nicolas had not called them. It is the only mercy those women will ever get. She reaches the young mother and takes the child from her; taken aback but grateful, the younger woman scrambles out, and they leave together, heels clicking on the hard floor.

The dead children so wonderfully risen totter past the staring music master, three quarters of the way up the aisle. Their bodies are barely cohering, their stench unbearable. To bring them back like this is the last shameful, sickening agony. Britten, Crozier, the school governors, all these ecumenical idiots should have stopped to *think*. An evil butcher seizes some Christian children, slaughters them, and offers them up to eat on his bill of fare. Who is that butcher going to be? A Jew, of course. It's a medieval story. The tenor up at the front, his eyes starting from his head, is bravely standing his ground; his voice has summoned up these terrors, and he has no idea what to do about them. The music master rises from his seat. He wants to scream. He wants to cover the children with blankets, make them decent and comprehensible like other refugees. But a refugee from death is an ungovernable horror. The border between death and life, surely, must remain firm, all others having been overrun?

The music master leaves his pew and follows the children. He is the only adult in the church, this whole time, who has chosen to move toward them. He towers over them. They were very young when they died. The two boys and the girl finally reach the altar. They are still, looking down as if defeated. The tenor and conductor stand, braced, dividing the dead children from the living, guarding the eight remaining choristers. Of the boy singers, four are weeping, two staring, one has eyes tight shut, one is kneeling, vomiting in a corner. The music master comes up to the naked children. They turn, seeming confused. He addresses them slowly, clearly, in one language after another, in all the languages he has spoken and read and translated over the past eight years, the languages that are still being written and spoken, day after day, into the depositions being made in the former camp at Dachau, even to this hour. He finds the ones that the children understand—not the same ones, among the three—and then he gestures at the choirmaster, at the living boys behind him. The man turns and issues a command in a cracked voice. Three boys, shaking with nerves, remove their surplices, leaving themselves standing, trembling, in their Virgin blue robes. The surplices hang in the choirmaster's hand like limp white nightgowns. Looking at them, the music master nearly breaks down. He snatches them and gives them to the dead children. They are helpless and inert and require his help in pulling them over their heads. Robed, they look even more pathetic. The music master and the two men on stage stare at each other in wonder and horror, in the mutual recognition of people somehow taking charge of an unthinkable situation. Speaking gently, calling, the music master leads the two boys and the girl, very slowly now, on the brink of dissolution, towards the door. He tries not to think of what will be left when they cross the threshold of Aldeburgh church: of how the pickled children will relapse into so much *pork*.

My Grandfather and the Archive of Insanity

> Next to his house was a piece of broken board
> which had: "TRESPASSERS W" on it. When
> Christopher Robin asked the Piglet what it
> meant, he said it was his grandfather's name, and
> had been in the family for a long time.
>
> —A. A. Milne, *The House at Pooh Corner*, 1928

Apophenia is the word for it. Patternicity. I'll come back to this later.

Neither of my grandfathers fought in the Second World War. They were both the right age for it. But both worked in what were deemed critical industries: one was the foreman in a cement factory, and one was a school principal and inspector of schools. Plenty of people agreed with the first exemption and many fewer with the last. On at least one occasion the school inspector grandfather was presented with a chicken's feather in the street. He was a nasty piece of work in a conventional sort of way, that grandfather, and little is going to be said here about the contents of his head. Rather, I'm going to talk about the other one. While the contents of his head were ridiculous, they were nonetheless interesting. He had a grade eight education. Of the two grandfathers, you'd think he would be the least likely to write a book—the other one

Sarah Tolmie

had a PhD in education—but that's not the way it worked out. Not that he ever finished his book. His project, which was supposed to be a genealogical history of the family, was like that history of whatever small Ontario town it is in the Alice Munro book—*Jubilee?*—the one written by somebody's uncle, that is so exhaustive as to be never-ending, including every trivial event in the town's archive without exception, such that the author never gets it past World War One or whatever his watershed year was, despite thirty years of his female relatives tiptoeing around him as he carried out his important *research*. After his retirement, my grandfather lived in a similar condition. His wife, my paternal grandmother, had been to Normal School and taught in a one-room schoolhouse before her marriage (though certainly, in the manner of those days, not after). She thus might have been in a position to question the veracity of some of my grandfather's wilder claims about the way the various MacThises, MacThatses, and Somethingies in our immediate and historical genealogy fit into the mythographic history of Scotland, the earliest and dimmest fables of which he accepted as out of whole cloth. But, as far as I know, she never did. She left him alone to accumulate a mad mass of books on the Highland Clearances, the economic history of Scotland, the law of feudal tenure, the works of Sir Walter Scott and Robbie Burns, Dr Johnson's itinerary through the Isles (at least part of which he once retraced with my bemused father in tow), eighteenth- and nineteenth-century nationalist translations of the major medieval Scots chroniclers, and ranging outward into Egyptology and the further reaches of Masonic occultism. These he displayed proudly, library-style, on units of metal shelving, five deep, in one wing of the finished basement that he used for his study, ordered strictly by some idiosyncratic method of his own devising that he kept in a handwritten and numbered catalogue. I remember this impressed me very much as a child: rows of books in matching dull red covers, some with Latin names. Thinking back on it now, it strikes me that my grandfather made no effort to make his library, in his private space, resemble a gentleman's library. There were no leather armchairs, shaded lamps, or built-in shelving lining the walls. He worked on a large bare table under stark overhead light. His book room was clearly modeled on a public library, books in utilitarian shelves, using the Dewey decimal system. Or perhaps a school library. These were his images of literate authority. (When his eldest son, a Rhodes scholar in medieval history, arrived at Oxford, it must have been quite a shock to the system.)

The jewel of his collection was what he called the Family Bible, a large-format early nineteenth-century print, made for the pulpit, which had births, deaths, and marriages inscribed on its front flyleaves dating from the 1840s to the 1870s or so; this he had obtained from the small Presbyterian church near the family farm when it closed down, its membership becoming consolidated into a larger United Church congregation. I still have this huge book, and it continues to impress me, even though it has suffered water damage from a flood in the late 1980s. Or perhaps its state of delicacy actually enhances it. He wrote to, and perhaps for, many genealogical research societies, and was in correspondence with parish offices and churchwardens and assorted local record keepers in the Hebrides and the northwest of Scotland, as well as in small towns in Ontario and Nova Scotia. All this, in combination with the eternal task of mowing the ludicrous amount of lawn that came with his retirement property, kept him very busy. Eventually he bought a ride-on mower, which I think reminded him of the tractors upon which he had spent his youth—he came from a farming family of ten siblings. Grow up trying to get grasses to grow high; die back trying to keep them short.

This sounds innocuous as far as it goes, all part of the hyper-vigilance most people exercise about their heritage if they live in Canada. But it has its weird and sinister aspects. By way of comparison, let us consider Alfred Watkins. He lived from 1855 to 1935 in Herefordshire, a generation before my grandfather. He invented ley lines, those ribbons of mystical force that ran under the ground and connected sites of commercial and ritual significance for the Neolithic people of the British Isles, if not the entire world. To this day, millions of people think they exist, and always have done, that they are a genuine feature of physical anthropology across the globe. Tour guides, hill-walkers, armchair mystics everywhere will tell you in all seriousness that Machu Picchu, Stonehenge, the Forbidden City, Shakespeare's birthplace, Watling Street, and the Apple headquarters in Silicon Valley are all located on leys, running in wonderfully straight lines, often radiating out like the spokes of a wheel from local sites of power. You can spot them from heights, as traces in the landscape; you can find them on maps by drawing straight lines through four or more culturally significant places; now there are apps for it. Everybody is interested in ancient human cultures; everybody wants to find ways in which the contemporary world is still connected to them. It is empowering to do your hiking not as a vulgar tourist but as a forensic investigator, crowd-sourcing details for a grand theory; it's cool to use compasses and pro-tractors—or apps—and take photographs that are evidential, not just selfies or nature porn. The idea that you, personally, can move along, document, or even discover, cosmic lines of force that conjoin nature and culture just by walking out your front door and proceeding through your city or suburb, or by heading out to remoter regions wherever they may be and looking at them with a critical eye: come on, it's fantastic. It's worked like a charm for a hundred years. Almost exactly a hundred years, in fact: it was in 1921 that Alfred Watkins, out walking in his home county, through familiar landscape, had an epiphany at perceiving that a number of important features of the terrain, all disparate but all, he posited, man-made, lined up perfectly. He had discovered, as he put it, his first ley line. He worked up his theory, first to a local audience of landscape enthusiasts in Herefordshire, tracing the significant relationships between ancient trackways, notched sight lines, moats, cists, marker stones, mounds, bits of Roman camps and other marginally legible objects in the landscape and the more obvious and familiar hilltops, church spires, wells, and bodies of water that people knew; the locals were ecstatic, happy to take the leap of faith—from the known back in time toward the unknown—with him. By 1925 he had written *The Old Straight Track: Its Mounds, Beacons, Moats, Sites and Mark Stones*, and ley lines were here to stay.

It is important to realize that Watkins' vision is pure crap. It's hallucinatory. It has no basis in fact whatsoever, as experts in the fields he rides roughshod over—geology, anthropology, linguistics, and many others—have said continually since the book came out. It's hobbit *feng shui*. Nonsense. And not the nonsense of logical play that you find in the work of his near-contemporary Lewis Carroll, the whimsical but deep inversions of category of a trained mathematician. Watkins' work is not about inversion; it's about accretion, the pile-up of facts, inferences, and free associations into a tissue of seemingly incontrovertible truth, impossible to argue with because composed of many discrete factual items shorn of their explanatory contexts freely admixed with pure projection. There are no clear categories. Chiefly, there is no clear distinction between inside and outside: namely, the inside and outside of Watkins' own head. Anything that he sees with his own eyes is a fact—more than a fact, an *observation*—regardless of the fact that what he sees is laced with presupposition: this stone is a sacrificial altar; this gap in the modern hedgerow is an ancient sightline to that sacred hilltop; the Old English word for hill (*hlaew*) is obviously related to the word *halo* (when, in fact, the latter comes from the Greek *halōs* and is completely unrelated), and so on. It's sheer bunkum. The theory of ley lines is not a theory, as Richard Dawkins would tell you with desperate patience, because it is not falsifiable. No new information can disprove it. *The Old Straight Track* is precisely the kind of fuzzy communication that drove Wittgenstein, at almost exactly the same time (the *Tractatus Logico-Philosophicus* came out in 1922) into the adamantly precise (but, as it turned out, equally vanishing) terms of symbolic logic early in his career. One glance at it would have given him yet another hernia.

My grandfather's book of family history was shaping up to be exactly like this. I know this only from hearsay, I admit, but I am pretty sure of my ground. I haven't seen his manuscript; I'm not even sure where it is. It might be sitting in an archive in a public library in the Peterborough region somewhere; it might have been purged long ago. One thing that emerges clearly in discussion with two of his sons, something that sounds like it's personal but that I diagnose retrospectively as generic, is that when it came to talking about family history—or indeed, about anything historical or intellectual—my grandfather was, as they both attest, "bloodyminded," "dogged," "argumentative," "illogical," "insistent." He had fixed views that he had worked out carefully, and to his own mind in a scholarly fashion, and on them he would not be moved. He did not accept corrections to his chain of evidence; facts that did not accord with his preconceived notions he would simply deny, no matter how well backed up they were. He was impervious to expertise. This was, I have heard them both say, maddening. It was also weird, in that in most other respects he was the mildest of men. But he had made up his own version of the world—or the world that he cared about—from the evidence of his books and correspondence, and it was unshakeable. He was, petty though it seems to say it, a case that corresponded perfectly to the old adage that a little learning is a dangerous thing.

He had apophenia. That is, he found patterns in things when they weren't there, or attributed systematic meaning to random coincidences of structure. I speak of this as though it were an illness, and in many ways it is: it's a rhetorical disease, one that is horribly prevalent today. It's the one that underlies conspiracy theories of all kinds. Its roots, I would argue, lie precisely in the period and the practices of people like my grandfather: in the early years of the twentieth century, when the bulk of the work of Victorian gentleman amateurs in what we now think of as the social sciences hit the popular reading public. Victorian male writers were tireless (as they had women doing all domestic work for them); they were persnickety, fact-gathering in their fields to the minutest degree and prepared to cite all of it, relevant or not; being both gentlemen, with access to privileged institutions and techniques of learning, and amateurs, therefore not really responsible to those institutions or speaking for them, their works often come across as purely personal achievements. They could effortlessly and silently rely on solid training in classical languages, in modern philology, in mathematics and logic, the baseline disciplines that enabled them to carry out their individual research, such that they were invisible to the less educated reader: the effect was, in brief, that what they said, went. Theirs was a scholarship of assertion. What my grandfather, reading these guys forty years later, could not ascertain was that this was a *style* of scholarship; it was a way for such privileged men to express their local results clearly and immediately, one that assumed no need to acknowledge all the basic training in reading, writing, and logic that underlay their ability to form arguments, verbal or mathematical. Underneath their breezy observations—which were tantamount to assertions most of the time—was the hidden work of scholarship: all the language-learning, memorization, comparison, amassing of concepts, manuscript study, evidence gathering, consultation, knowledge of previous sources, evolution of tools, and so on that made their work meaningful (and falsifiable). All this business went on under the hood of their prose and did not exist for my grandfather and men like him. Scholarship, in fact, was not really a thing for them, just as it is not now for many people. It wasn't even a matter of conscious skepticism; it was simple blindness. Thus, let's say, a man like Alfred Watkins could imply that when he looked at such-and-such a monument in X, Herefordshire, and was reminded of statues of Hermes—one man looking at one statue and comparing it off-the-cuff to one or two he remembers seeing in a museum or a book somewhere—he was making a comparison as meaningful as one that his contemporary, the Cambridge codicologist M. R. James, might make about a decorative motif shared between Anglo-Saxon and insular Latin manuscripts. No. James could prove it: he could find and name the manuscripts; he could adduce dozens or hundreds more out of the thousands he had seen, described, and catalogued. He could read the languages and scripts concerned. Watkins' statement is a reminiscence, part of a travelogue, and that is all.

It was in this thoroughly erroneous spirit that my grandfather set out to write his history. I doubt there was anything hubristic in it when he set out, when it was a detail-oriented, small-scale, fact-gathering matter of putting together who had married whom; who had come to Canada aboard what ships; what their jobs had been before and after; who had farmed what farms. What he might have said about title to such farms and expropriation of native land I, fortunately, have no idea; had the topic come up at all, I expect we might have heard a few remarks on social Darwinism. Be that as it may have been, where it would all have fallen apart—and he and my uncle, the future medievalist, had several of their most lasting arguments about this—was how he grafted this prosaic, and probably quite correct, genealogical history onto the larger history of Scotland. For, once he had got the family safely back on to Scottish shores, how could he stop there? Surely they had to have taken part in the great dramas, the endless wars with England, the Auld Alliance?—and then, how had the Scots people, the nation (as completely distinct from the English, the Irish, and the Welsh) ever come to be on the island of Britain in the first place? What shape had their migration taken? You can see how, seeing himself and his family already as part of a diaspora, this might have been a pressing question.

Sarah Tolmie

There is an answer to this question, and it is insane. It can be found in the earliest Scots chroniclers like John of Fordun and Hector Boece. My grandfather had these Latin works, or parts of them, in translation. To him they were gospel. From them he got the story of the eponymous Scota, daughter of an Egyptian pharaoh, ultimate ancestor of all Scots. He also read, in those chroniclers and their Victorian translators, of waves of Celtic migration into Europe from Scythia—in other words, from Asia Minor—of which the proto-Scots formed a part, thus proving their immemorial antiquity as a people. Older than Greeks. Far older than Romans. As old as ancient, tribal Jews, and like them, mixed up with Egypt, the other great civilization of the ancient world, as Europeans saw it. But chiefly—and this is the part that my grandfather flatly refused to understand, to the fury of my frustrated uncle—this combined narrative makes Scots older than Trojans. This is the historiographical kicker. In the English origin story, put about by Geoffrey of Monmouth in the twelfth-century *History of the Kings of Britain*, the English, or Britons, are descended from the eponymous Brutus, a companion of Aeneas fleeing the Trojan war. People repeated this myth steadily until the eighteenth century. Almost all nations in Europe claimed a Trojan ancestor; it was one of the underpinnings of the European community. By the fourteenth century, dynastic complications in the feudal regime of Scotland—one profoundly intermarried with the English aristocracy and trying to refute claims about English overlordship of the kingdom—made it necessary to go one better: to come up with a foundation myth that proved its royal dynasties and its people were ancient and distinct, and in fact, pre-Trojan. Hence, the Scota story. It was actually an interesting step out of line, and one cherished by independence-minded Scots historiographers for centuries thereafter. Such historical exigencies cut no ice with my grandfather. The fact that people had particular and changeable goals when they wrote their histories, ones quite different from his, simply did not compute. The fact that most medieval chronicles, at least those parts about the mythical origins of nations, were convenient lies, was unthinkable. History was an objective science. The Scota story was true: true enough to be transferred nearly verbatim for hundreds of years through generations of chroniclers. It was a discrete factual nugget as solid as a chunk dug out of a mine, a set of facts worth repeating. And every repetition increased its truth value; each iteration could be cross-referenced and traced. He had gone through the exercise of tracing it through many of its multiple attestations, back and back and back through the chronicle tradition, and thus, personally, proved it. He had succumbed to the joy of pattern recognition. The fact that a big lie gains traction the more it is repeated would have struck him, in this context, as obscene.

The final nail in the coffin on any rationality about this material came in the form of a bad etymology, much like those that litter Watkins' *The Old Straight Track*. Somewhere along the line my grandfather learned that some of the late Hellenistic pharaohs were named *Ptolemy*. Once he had learned that the P was silent in English, he was able to discover a homonym for his own name, *Tolmie*. As the entire enterprise on which he had set out was to provide the history of this name, I imagine that this similarity—or imagined identity—struck him with colossal force. I bet he had an epiphany similar to that of Watkins on that day in 1921 when he saw the landscape magically line up before him. He had, at a stroke, brought his genealogical history to its termination point: here was the Egyptian origin of the Scots name Tolmie. His family could thus be brought, dramatically and uncontrovertibly, into kinship with Scota, daughter of pharaoh.

There is no etymological or historical relationship between *Tolmie* and *Ptolemy*, any more than there is between *hlaew* and *halo*. The Gaelic name *Tolmach*, probably a toponym meaning by-the-hillock (*tolm*), comes into English as *Tolmie*. This has nothing to do with the Ptolemaic pharaohs, whose surname comes from a common Greek personal name, *Ptolemaeus*. The fact that a few pretentious people—bets are they were Masons, like my grandfather, full of weird ideas about Hellenistic Egypt—in the eighteenth century spelled their Gaelic name *Ptolemy* does not change this fact. But my grandfather went to his grave claiming kinship with Cleopatra nonetheless, for the greater glory of his clan.

As a coda to this tale, I should mention that my uncle, while studying at Oxford in the 1950s, went to the British Museum and acquired, in their surprisingly expansive gift shop, a late Roman seal—though in our family it is often referred to as a coin—that bears the name of Ptolemy. In the spirit of irony, no doubt, after years of futile arguing with him, he sent this ancient object to my grandfather. By him it was received, unironically, as a precious family memento. He hoarded it in his study next to the volumes of Scottish chronicle that he was certain were related to it. My father inherited this small black object. He treats it in exactly the same way and likewise regales anybody he can get to stand still with the wonderful facts of our family connection to the pharaohs of Egypt. I, like my uncle before me, am a medievalist—I even wrote my thesis on medieval Scots historiography—and I have tried to explain to him that this is not true. It makes no difference at all.

The Wittgenstein Finds

The world is everything that is the case.

—Ludwig Wittgenstein,
The Tractatus Logico-Philosophicus,
Proposition 1 (1922)

The grave of Wittgenstein receives fewer visitors than that of Jim Morrison. Wittgenstein fandom is an altogether quieter thing. The use of the word *fan* in connection to himself, of course, would have made Wittgenstein positively bilious. Or perhaps, more bilious than he normally was: a spare, ascetic sort of man at all times, he had a nervous stomach, indeed a nervous everything. People who knew him well suspected that he was allergic to reality. They would watch him staring bleakly at his plate in hall at Trinity College, surrounded by embarrassed undergraduates who would have preferred him to be anywhere else—such as, for instance, up at High Table with the rest of the Fellows—and say to themselves, ah, there it is again. You really make it hard on yourself, Ludwig, old boy.

Cambridge guidebooks will tell you that the philosopher Ludwig Wittgenstein (fl. 1889-1951) is buried in the cemetery of the Ascension, on the northwestern edge of Cambridge, just off the Huntingdon Road. The establishment is Church of England but prides itself on accommodating every kind of nonconformist under its sod, religious or secular. The university has always thrown these up by dozens; the parish returns them decently to the ground. Wittgenstein, who identified at varying times of his life as a Jew, a Catholic, and an agnostic, separately or together, and never conventionally, in this respect fits right in. In the end he received, after his death from prostate cancer at the age of 62, a Catholic burial.

Wittgenstein, it must be said, now lies in the ground perilously near the birthplace of quite another breed of Nonconformist: namely, Oliver Cromwell. Cromwell was born in the village of Huntingdon in 1599, and the fact that there is a cemetery that admits Catholics, never mind Jews or agnostics, anywhere in the neighborhood drives him apoplectic. Students at Sidney Sussex College, where Cromwell's head is buried, hear him yelling stifled imprecations against popish ceremonies at all hours, especially during Lent, to which he seems to have a particular objection. Wittgenstein's fortunately distinctive name has never been mentioned specifically, however, as far as they can tell; students admit that, as a rule, they have trouble making out the Lord Protector's seventeenth-century English. It may be that, up to this point, Cromwell has failed to notice Wittgenstein.

It is well known in many circles that the celebrated dead of Cambridge, virtuous or infamous, continue their debates under the ground. Members of the Moral Sciences Club, in particular, simply carry on *post mortem* as standard practice. Why should death stop them? A dry susurration is heard clear across the town from its several graveyards, and from beneath the pavements of chapels, almost every evening. This phenomenon is explained away by the canny locals as wind from the fens lest it upset anxious tourists. The worst midnight moaning is attributed to cattle—Cambridge being, as everyone who has been there knows, a town much haunted by cows.

Wittgenstein, a silent man in later life, is silent in death. Up to the present time there has been no evidence of his participation in the underground intellectual forum. It is believed by some who know his work that he objects to it on principle: an underground being, traditionally, an elite formation. Surrounded as he presently is by numerous members of the chattering classes—Frazer, for example, always windy and buried nearby, is still to be heard listing corrigenda for the final edition of *The Golden Bough*, and Cockcroft, who, though quiet for the most part, is not infrequently consulted by members of the Atomic Energy Authority at moments of crisis—Wittgenstein can be imagined lying laconically by, surrounded by gossiping Darwins, taciturn as a hero from one of his beloved classic westerns. It may also be the case that having pointed out, memorably, that *death is not an event of life*, that it is not *lived through* (and is thus not legitimately subject to discussion by the living), he has felt it inapposite to say anything. Perhaps his stern belief in this state of affairs has prevented his doing so. Perhaps he is absent; he has willed himself away, refusing to overstep the boundary of the delicate mysticism that characterized his later life, determined not to say too much. Others have objected to this possibility on the grounds of his equally memorable statement that "the world is not subject to my will," preferring to think of him, amid the ranting and prosing of the dead professoriate, as maintaining a strained but compassionate silence. Gauntlet Purefoy Huddleston (fl. 1877-1916), Captain in the Royal Engineers, who has become rather a spokesperson for the population at Ascension—he has jokingly referred to himself as "the herald"—has had only this to say on the matter of Wittgenstein: *yes, of course he's here. Read the stone.* Absence and presence are touchy categories for Capt. Huddleston, whose earthly remains lie in Flanders at Elverdinghe. He is represented in the cemetery by his name on a family monument. *You don't honestly think it's the bodies that are talking, do you?* he has said, rather testily, on another occasion.

⁀

Wittgenstein has thus, regrettably, not been the author of any posthumous aphorisms. Much to the chagrin of his followers, neither has he ventured any observations on the language games of the dead. These would be invaluable. Nonetheless, constituencies among his fandom—the credulous, according to some, the materialist, according to others—have recently put forth the theory that he is beginning to communicate. How? By means of physical objects. "Wittgenstein was always attentive to the status of objects. He appreciated their enigma. After all, he set out to train as an engineer," says metaphysician Dr Cornelis Opdinge. "You might even say that in some ways he anticipated the claims of today's Object-Oriented Ontologists. Maybe it's wishful thinking, but that's why I find myself willing to accept that he would choose this mode of communication."

Dr Opdinge's speculations arose, along with those of many other Wittgenstein experts, shortly after the refurbishment of Wittgenstein's memorial slab in 2015. This modest stone, incised only with his name and dates, had become covered with lichen due to its shaded and damp position; likewise, its letters had faded and become difficult to read. The stone was cleaned and its letters re-incised and repainted: it was a meticulous and professional intervention by all accounts, carried on with a modest sort of fanfare suitable to the occasion. Shortly there-after—in August of 2015, to be exact—an eighteenth-century, silver-gilt menorah was found protruding out of the ground at the upper left quadrant of the grave (the area closest to the heart, notes Dr Victoria Stein, professor of the philosophy of emotion at St Crux). The precious object was battered and covered in an admixture of earth from Cambridgeshire and Vienna, Wittgenstein's birthplace. Scholarship and sleuthing by interested parties at Cambridge and elsewhere eventually revealed that it had been part of the historic collection on display in the now-lost Palais Wittgenstein in Argentinierstrasse; it may once have belonged to the family of Wittgenstein's maternal grandfather. "Karl Wittgenstein, captain of industry and Ludwig Wittgenstein's father, was a strict Catholic and raised his children so, but he was also an ardent collector of *objets d'art* and liturgical silver, some of which reflected his Jewish heritage," writes Datura Franklin in an informal *catalogue raisonné* that includes the object, which goes on: "We would never associate such an ornate object with the modernist aesthetic of the Haus Wittgenstein, for example, that severe white box that Wittgenstein helped to design for his sister from 1926-29, but it's important to realize that the young Wittgenstein grew up surrounded by turn-of-the-century opulence. If the engraved K on the base does stand for Kalmus or Koppelman, Bohemian family names associated with Leopoldine, Wittgenstein's mother—the piece is from the workshop of the early eighteenth-century master Gottfried Imlin in Prague—then we could be looking at some kind of statement about her. Childhood nostalgia? A profession of loyalty? It appears that she was a timorous woman who suffered under domestic tyranny. Or, on the other hand, is its extrusion from the grave a form of rejection, a condemnation of decadent form, or of the Jewish religion? Could Wittgenstein be self-identifying as a *Bohemian?*"

This valuable object, temporarily on loan to the Victoria and Albert Museum but legally returned to the custody of the Wittgenstein family, has invited many such speculations. Cynics immediately claimed it as a hoax, saying that it had obviously been planted in the grave, or even left, as innumerable objects had been before, as a gift or memento by the graveside. There is no CCTV at the site, and there was immediate clamor for some to be set up, in the event that any other items should surface. After a lengthy review by the Dead Intellectuals Department (DID), the branch of the National Trust that deals with the Cambridge phenomenon and its Oxford counterpart, and those few in other parts of the United Kingdom, it was agreed that the grave and its immediate area could be subject to remote surveillance for a period of six months, applicable rights to privacy being temporarily waived. This was deemed more suitable than mounting a 24-hour guard, as potentially more damaging to the property. Though trying to keep a low profile, a DID van was to be found parked in the laneway at regular intervals (their motto—*Quare furor est futurus*—on the side was a bit of a giveaway).

꩜

Within weeks there was another find. This one was more macabre and upped the ante considerably on the mystery as a whole. No one was seen planting it. More people than usual came and went from the grave site, but none were seen to dig or disturb the earth in any way. In the first week of September, a small ivory patch appeared in the upper right quadrant of the site, very close to the edge of the slab. After the elapse of several days, another whitish patch appeared alongside it, hugging the edge of the slab; then a third. All three rose slowly, wriggling or rotating subtly—which fact could be seen if CCTV footage was sped up—until they were perhaps two centimeters out of the ground. There they stayed. DID personnel whispered among themselves that these looked like fragments of bone; they were uncertain what to do; they consulted some forensic pathologists and the Archbishop of Canterbury. The latter advised them to proceed with disinterment. In due course, and with due care, three tiny bones were raised from the earth. They were phalanges. People looked at them with curiosity and horror, wondering if Wittgenstein himself was trying to clamber out of his grave. There was a move to have his body exhumed and examined, but it was vetoed by the family.

A visiting musicologist, in Cambridge for an unrelated reason, heard about the find. He was shown the bones. Fingers, he thought, and a dim light went on in his mind—Wittgenstein? It couldn't be. It can't be, he thought. Can it? He made a suggestion to the DID men. Family permission was sought, DNA gathered. The finger bones proved to be those of Paul Wittgenstein, Ludwig's brother, a famous concert pianist who had lost his right arm in the First World War. There was no keeping this out of the hands of the media. Headlines screamed and phones lit up across the planet. The whole cemetery had to be cordoned off. Nights, there was so much talk underground that the murmur could be heard hundreds of meters away, as if people were standing next to a call center. There was a constant police presence in the Huntingdon Road, to the great annoyance of the colleges at that end of town. The family was understandably upset.

How had the bones come there? How had they ever been found? From what strange burial pit had they been unearthed? Or had they—the thought was appalling—been sitting in some ghoulish display? A hospital museum? A kinky music collector? Had the finger bones of Paul Wittgenstein been handed down, father to son, in some family somewhere, ever since 1916? Had they been bought and sold as curiosities, like Cromwell's head? The bones were immediately surrendered to the Wittgenstein family for re-interment, with profuse DID apologies, though the DID was unsure exactly what it was apologizing for.

⌇

It could not possibly have been Wittgenstein who had done this, his admirers thought. It was far too vulgar. He would have gone to the ends of the Earth to avoid such a spectacle. But then, speculated some, maybe being *in* the Earth was just as far as that: maybe priorities changed there. He had never been one to talk about his family. But, psychologists reasoned, like everyone, he had *had* a family. A very difficult one, by all accounts. Was this an attempt at reconciliation? After all, he had shucked off the family fortune, moved to another country. What was he saying about his brother Paul? Could it be a commendation of his World War One service? His own had been exemplary, earning medals for valor. Or could it be a condemnation of such uncivilized practices, worthy only of burying in the ground? And why Paul? There had been three other brothers, all suicides. They had bones. Was Ludwig extolling his brother Paul for rising to the challenge of staying alive—a task he had personally found nearly insurmountable?

Or, as theologians speculated avidly, was Wittgenstein taking a position on the resurrection of the flesh? Maimonides had included it as a key tenet of Judaism; it occurs in the books of Isaiah and Daniel; medieval Christians had believed in it. Yet it has been a divisive theological point in modernity. "It seems to me more than possible that Wittgenstein is making an ecumenical gesture in this," opined Alfred Wiggle, newly inducted Canon of Westminster. "We might consider it typical of him, a man of deep but unconventional religious feeling. He returns the bones of his brother to him as an eschatological token, a promise of future bodily resurrection. Potentially a promise to us all, Christian and Jew alike."

It was a taunt, some said meanly: *look, Paul, think how much better a piano player you would have been with these.*

Everybody waited for number three. Third time's the charm. Two could be a coincidence. Mind you, so could three. It could still be a random series of events. Three times in a row could still be random, technically. Like dice falling, lightning striking, whatever. Why can't Wittgenstein just talk like the rest of these gasbags? Come on, Ludwig. Stop being such a diva.

Entire books were written about the matter in philosophy departments, in many sub-disciplines—thirty-two in all, a testament to the broad appeal of his philosophy—as well as in cognate fields (literature, psychology, media, design, religious studies, even self-help) before there was any further activity at Wittgenstein's grave. Fans thought it likely that he was waiting for the media circus to subside. They tried to be patient. It is an awkward thing, being a Wittgenstein fan. One is always aware that one is succumbing to a cult of personality, when that personality would rigorously deny, and indeed anxiously shrink from, the very idea of a cult of personality. It is precisely this that one admires. Of course, this is perverse. It becomes inappropriate to admit to fandom at all. The only thing to do is to persevere in examining with a kind of silent doggedness the surprising range of questions that his work explores, much as he did himself. The fact that many of them peter out into dead ends, or are suddenly blocked off by the intrusion of the infinite—always a danger in Wittgenstein's thought—is, weirdly, often the reward. Thinking was, for Wittgenstein, fundamentally something one has to get over. Or get through. It's the state one is in afterward for which he was aiming. A kind of repose. It was a comical and touching goal for such an overwrought man. "That's the funny thing about this," wrote Maeve Middleton on her blog *Mountain Climber, Wittgenstein Reader* during this interval, "I feel that all this waiting around is intrinsically part of Wittgenstein's act of communication. He said, didn't he, that his work was *meant to be read slowly*? It's now that we're meant to be doing the work of philosophy: now that he's not speaking. We're supposed to be putting the objects, the utterances, together, trying to see how they relate—do they make a grammar, or what? What's the logic? Are they a binary pair? Does one continue the other? Of course, we'd all like a larger sample, but why should it be that easy? No language game is simple. Certainly this one he seems to have put us all into isn't—what even is it? Investigation? Divination? Wish fulfillment? And you know what I wonder? The menorah, the finger bones of his brother—are they *atomic facts*? Tautologies? Things that are themselves? If so, what's the response? Shock and awe, ladies and gentlemen, shock and awe."

~

When the next item worked its way out of the soil, it was a cell phone from the year 2000. Many fans were bitterly disappointed. It was the kind of thing they might have expected from Marshall McLuhan, not Wittgenstein. "Well, at least it's a kind of millenarian object, isn't it? A mobile phone? Probably the most revered and reviled object on Earth. That gives us something to work with, especially in combination with the other elements revealed so far," argued Kristov Zygorsky, chair of media studies at Mtsensk, in an interview at the time. The phone itself, an early Wokia, was whisked away by the DID. It remained at a forensics lab, location undisclosed, for eleven months. Wittgenstein fans perked up: the phone obviously had a complex story attached to it. The internet was wild with theories. (One interesting sidelight was #burythephone, a meme that had considerable currency throughout 2018. It brought Wittgenstein's work to the attention of a whole new generation of readers.) Meanwhile, analytical and other philosophers tried to make sense of the collocation of revealed objects, now that they had a third term. The question was, everybody said, one of framing. Should the items be construed grammatically, as in a sentence—and if so, what were the syntactical relationships (especially as all three items, on the face of it, were nouns)? Or in terms of symbolic logic? Should the objects be placed in an ontological hierarchy? Should they be studied sociologically, as evidences or predictors of behavior? Psychologically, was this a moment to free associate? Most importantly, did the three items make a closed set? If more were forthcoming, would all the data have to be dynamically re-analyzed? Was there any point to this at all?

(Was there any point to this at all? Of course there was. There is philosophy and then there is death. Indeed, this particular case suggests that philosophy outclasses death.)

Others took a different tack. They tried to address the communicative act as a mode. It was tendentious to try to identify motives for a dead speaker, not knowing anything about his circumstances, of course, so they tried their best to bracket these off. In general, why would Wittgenstein communicate—if that is what he was doing—by adducing objects, instead of using words, as his dead Cambridge compatriots did? People came up with various hypotheses:

1. He had despised his university colleagues in life and did not want to do what they did; he might do the same in death

2. He existed in a status that rendered speech impossible, perhaps some kind of terminal nonconformity, one greater than even the Church of England's most liberal graveyard could accommodate

3. All recent communications with him had come in the form of objects, tokens left by the graveside; he was responding in kind, continuing a language game that had already been initiated in its own terms

4. He was performing an end-run around the problem of reference, one that had continuously troubled his philosophy

5. It was an homage, ironical or serious, to Voltaire, whose philosophers on the floating island of Laputa had done the same thing in order to perform the operation described in number 4

6. He was continuing the discursive mode he had initiated many years previously by using a poker as a philosophical argument in a debate with Karl Popper.

The third possibility listed above caused considerable excitement. A large and diverse collection of items that had been left by or on the burial slab existed in the care of the parish. This included books, college scarves, keys, phones, food, candles, coins in many currencies, diverse small tools associated with engineering, small objects possibly associated with the Cambridge Apostles and believed to be sex toys, and so on. The most distinctive was a floor tile from the Palais Wittgenstein itself, probably obtained during its destruction in 1950; somebody must have brought it all the way from Vienna and laid it there in commemoration. Surely all of these were acts of communication? Perhaps the people concerned thought they were purely phatic, or that they were talking to themselves—but what if Wittgenstein had heard them?

⁒

"This is great, this is just great, this is very exciting," babbled a young woman who was never identified into the DID camera in March of 2018 as she laid a crocheted bookmark reverently on Wittgenstein's slab. "I'm just leaving this here, you know, not because I imagine he's literally reading down there, but just as a way of saying, you know, hello? maybe take a pause in your train of thought, you know, put a pin in it and acknowledge that I'm here? See me in some way as your…uh, fan? I mean, I know it's perishable, but then I'm perishable, too, and surely that's all part of it, the difference in our statuses: him dead and me living and yet we might still be talking. It seems amazing that we can communicate, I mean, that I can talk to Wittgenstein, how amazing is that? Wow. You never know, but maybe this bookmark will be the next prompt; maybe it will spawn some kind of utterance or thing or whatever. Of course, I won't be here to hear it, not directly—I mean not if it comes ten years from now or something—but you know, I'll feel like I'm part of the chain. I mean, when you think about it, who knows which of these gifts that get left he's responding to? If it's a question-and-answer thing, how can we figure out who he said "menorah" to? I mean, jeez, what kind of object would have to have been left for the answer to be "my brother's finger bones"? When was *that* question asked, and what with? I mean, he's been here since 1951. What if it was that very same year, and now everybody's here in 2018 wondering what the fuck's with the finger bones, you know, like it was some universal statement. Wittgenstein, you know, I'm always telling people he's not a guru, not my guru or whatever, he's a real philosopher, he's not Luke Skywalker. We don't have to take every single sentence as the ultimate truth, I mean, Jesus, he'd hate that. No. But now that I'm actually here…I guess what I'm wondering is, how exactly do you make laying out your gift, your significant object, umm…interrogative?"

The phone had been the detonator for a bomb exploded by the Real IRA on 1 June, 2000, on Hammersmith Bridge, London. This bleak fact emerged thirteen months after the phone had worked its way out of the ground at the foot of the observation site and then disappeared into DID investigative hands. It was the DID who made the announcement. Their sources were never revealed. The National Secrets Act was cited. Freakishly, the phone, though damaged and soaked, had survived the blast; it had been thrown clear into the Thames.

Nobody had been killed in the explosion. What statement Wittgenstein sought to make with such an object was an open question. It was borderline offensive. Possibly subversive. How had he gotten hold of it, as it had been, as the DID dispassionately described it, in police custody? "I dunno if he dematerialized it or what, but I can't think of any other way it could've got outta there," said a mystified security guard at a secure storage location. For the first time, the graveside phenomenon took on a political dimension. All the CCTV footage was reviewed; many people were convinced that it had been hacked, and that the Wittgenstein Finds had all been planted by a person or persons unknown. For the first time, the name Wittgenstein trended pejoratively; anti-intellectual, anti-Semitic, homophobic, and right-wing nationalist slurs were thrown around. Cambridge University issued a statement in his defense. The DID, in consultation with the parish council, mounted a rota of volunteers to guard the memorial against defacement or other interference. There were scuffles, and a number of arrests were made.

Did this mean that Ludwig Wittgenstein was a representative of—what?—the Eternal IRA? His philosophy had been resolutely apolitical. While never being a pacifist of the Bertrand Russell stripe, active in both World Wars, as a decorated soldier of the Austro-Hungarian empire in the First and a volunteer hospital orderly in London in the Second, he had never shown the slightest interest in factional politics or postcolonial freedom-fighting. He had become a British citizen in 1938. "I think people are looking at this the wrong way," explained Benjamin Cooper, ethics specialist, to a national newspaper: "Wittgenstein died in 1951. The man barely used the postal service. His orientation was anti-science, anti-gadget. Lots of people think breakthroughs in communication technology are the ultimate signs of progress. He was suspicious of progress. Think about it: now we say *my phone blew up*, meaning it's full of juicy news—he's pointing out that they are used in literal explosions, weaponized into IEDs. I note also that nobody was killed in this bombing. To me that counts for something; it suggests Wittgenstein was squeamish about the whole idea."

"We need to look at the object: the power of the object, the potentialities of the object," argued Hilaire Grégoire, author of *Objets idéologiques*: "We need to get back to that, and sidestep these sensationalist claims. This phone, it seems almost a misstep on the philosopher's part, if I'm being honest. We should keep in mind that this is the first object he's adduced that post-dates his own death. And it does so by a considerable period: there's a lot of distance between 1951 and 2018. It's possible he is out of touch."

Maeve Middleton, on her blog, summed it up it this way: "Of course, we'll never know for certain. But Wittgenstein gave up on certainty early in his career. At the end of the day, when I look at it, I see a warning. Basically, beware the phone. This sounds dumb, I realize. But bear with me: I think he's prefaced his statement that the phone is a double-edged sword today with a complex statement of identity, one that points out his own limitations as a speaker. He's structured the whole, we might say, as an anecdote. So, to me—and this is my blog so I can do what I want here, even if it's a bit of a stretch—the statement that we have so far is roughly this: *I, Wittgenstein* (this is the name on the gravestone, the first object, the one that nobody seems to talk about—and isn't it interesting that this whole business began when this name was re-inscribed?), *being the kind of man who comes from a household that displayed this silver-gilt menorah* (meaning rich, meaning Viennese, meaning specifically the Palais Wittgenstein, meaning as part of a collection for display rather than in practical use, thus also meaning something about religious affiliation or layering of faiths) *and having this kind of brother* (Paul Wittgenstein, a concert pianist despite having only one arm, a war survivor, a survivor in general, being the only other son in the family who didn't kill himself, in some respects a proxy for Ludwig himself as a brilliant, maimed but determined individual, literalizing his metaphor of *family resemblance*) *warn you that this ubiquitous object, the mobile phone* (did you know that several phones were left as gifts by the grave over the years?) *is dangerous* (it can be made into a bomb). That's it, that's my shot at it. Make of it what you will."

☙

Perhaps belatedly, the controversial semiotician Alexandre Frotte contributed the remarks below, excerpted from his posthumously published collection, *Annoyances*:

"A famous philosopher begins to send up objects, as it were, from the underworld. In life he had been an obsessive man, once garrulous, then laconic. He would hardly do such a thing casually. Consider the pedagogical situation: the master speaks to the students from an altered state, drawing from an invisible reservoir. He is *deep*. So far this is conventional. Perhaps he is acting as a psychopomp, introducing his followers to the wisdom of death. He is saying to them, I am so far ahead of you that I'm actually dead. Wittgenstein was obsessed with death. He grew up surrounded by suicides; they were in vogue in the Vienna of his youth. Everyone was doing it. He failed at it, as he did at a number of other Viennese activities: he did not become a musician, or a psychoanalyst. He did not become a modern architect. He did not become an engineer, as his father had done, making millions; though he designed a jet engine at the age of nineteen, technology was not advanced enough to sustain his designs. He tried to be a sculptor, but produced only one piece, a bust of his sister Margaret, sponsor of the Haus Wittgenstein, itself a failed experiment that the family quickly sold. We may look upon this bust, *Head of a Girl*—it was sold in 2017 for €80,000—as the equivalent of the fragment of poetry composed by Socrates as he was waiting for execution. Socrates said that his mantic sign—that common Greek superstition, as naïve as having a guardian angel or a pet rock—had suggested to him that perhaps he had been practicing the wrong profession all along and that he should try something new. Thus with Wittgenstein: surrounded by artists, many of whom were his father's dependents, he made one attempt to succeed—to succeed in joining the Secession—but it didn't take. Wittgenstein could not be Viennese. He could not be a Wittgenstein. He left, professionless. Perhaps we ought to consider these objects he has been proffering to us in this light, as signs of his lost professions: not a rabbi, not a Catholic collector of silver; not a concert pianist, despite having perfect pitch; not a terrorist, though a man who wanted to destroy philosophy. Beginning in engineering, yet wanting to get down below its foundations; continuing in mathematics, yet still desiring to go deeper, to expose its roots in logic; running through logic, to arrive, hopelessly, at its end: Wittgenstein's trajectory was always *downward*. Inevitably, he continues his explorations now from below the ground, beneath our feet. Consider, also, the monument itself, his last design—indeed, his final sculpture, the companion piece to *Head* *of a Girl*, the remarkably successful *Body of a Man*—which is notable for its horizontality. Flat, low to the ground, on a single plane; it bears, as he would have said, a *family resemblance* to the man lying below it. Also spare and clear, modern, like the Haus Wittgenstein, but again, more successful: the *true* Haus Wittgenstein, a place of perfect silence, perfect repose. And if we were, for some perverse reason, to rear it up and stand it on its end, as if it were a man upright, where would our gaze fall, at eye level?* On the name Wittgenstein. Wittgenstein. The forename Ludwig, above, is an excrescence, like the dates below. It is as if the word denotes a profession, or a status, like Cooper or Tailor or Beloved Son, not a name. Names, he pointed out, have no real reference; they are hollow; they are placeholders for a vague congeries of associations. (The name, you may recall, that he chose for this stripping-away of meaning was *Moses*, the name of the patriarch in his own family who first took the name *Wittgenstein*.) Or, this word, *Wittgenstein*, which is so obviously the rhetorical center of the monument, might it be a verb? To Wittgenstein: an action, a performance, a way of being. Or even a command: Wittgenstein! Be Wittgenstein! Go forth, you, the beholder, and Wittgenstein with the best of them. There is, after all, no other way to describe exactly what it was that he did. To describe him as an anti-philosopher is paltry and insufficient. Wittgenstein. There it is. Wittgenstein. His last and best tautology."

Neither Middleton's nor Frotte's analyses were the last of their kind. Monographs are still being written about the

---

* Not having been to the grave myself and thus unsure of its dimensions, it might be that we would have to be kneeling in such a situation. He would have despised this posture. Let us hope it would not be necessary.

Wittgenstein Finds. Careers are being made. Philosophy is never over. However, no further objects have emerged from Wittgenstein's grave in the years since. In 2020, the DID stood down its surveillance and its personnel, transferring most of its effort to policing the graves of several celebrated epidemiologists in the London area, which had become sites of heavy traffic. The *Quare furor est futurus* van disappeared from the laneway. The Ascension parish council, however, keeps up a round-the-clock guard just in case, sustained by funds contributed from numerous national and international Wittgenstein societies. Philosophy students often contribute their time *pro bono* to this effort. Each one wants to be there in the event that there is a new addition to everything that is the case.

Acknowledgments

I began working on this book after reading Helen Marshall's *The Gold Leaf Executions*, which I was asked to blurb. It was immediately galvanizing. Helen then provided feedback on the manuscript in progress, for which I thank her. She also put me on to the work of M. John Harrison, whose novel *The Sunken Land Begins to Rise Again* proved sustaining of its later sections. Robert MacFarlane's introduction to the 2014 reissue of *The Old Straight Track* is the source of most of my information about Alfred Watkins in "My Grandfather and the Archive of Insanity." Also, Tanis MacDonald's book *Straggle: Adventures in Walking While Female* (2022) encouraged me to experiment with the voice of memoir in that particular story. All text from M. R. James's stories is drawn from Project Gutenberg. I would also like to thank Tony Walker of Classic Ghost Stories (YouTube) and Peter Yearsley of Librivox for audio recordings of M. R. James's stories, and Greg Wagland of Magpie Audio (YouTube) for audio recordings of Conan Doyle's Holmes stories. *Honey, Honey, Lion!* is the title of an illustrated children's book by Jan Brett; "Swish and Flick," as many people will recognize, is part of the spell *Accio* (Latin for "I fetch it" or "I summon it") in J. K Rowling's Harry Potter series. Both are quoted in the story "Honey Business."

ST, Kitchener, 2022

About the Author

This is Sarah Tolmie's sixth book with Aqueduct Press: others include *The Stone Boatmen*, nominated for the Crawford Award in 2015, and *The Little Animals*, winner of the Special Citation at the Philip K Dick Awards in 2020. In addition to publishing short fiction, novellas, and novels with Aqueduct, she has released two novellas with Tor.com, *The Fourth Island* and *All the Horses of Iceland*; the latter was listed as one of the top fantasy books of 2022 by *The New York Times*. She has also written three volumes of poetry for McGill-Queen's University Press; the second one, *The Art of Dying*, was a finalist for the 2019 Griffin Prize for Poetry. In her other life she is a Professor of English at the University of Waterloo. Her website is http://sarahtolmie.ca/.